The New York Times

IN THE HEADLINES

Due Process

DEFINING FAIR LEGAL TREATMENT

I0808543

THE NEW YORK TIMES EDITORIAL STAFF

Published in 2021 by New York Times Educational Publishing in association with The Rosen Publishing Group, Inc.
29 East 21st Street, New York, NY 10010

First Edition

The New York Times
Caroline Que: Editorial Director, Book Development
Phyllis Collazo: Photo Rights/Permissions Editor
Heidi Giovine: Administrative Manager

Rosen Publishing
Megan Kellerman: Managing Editor
Meredith Day: Editor
Greg Tucker: Creative Director
Brian Garvey: Art Director

Cataloging-in-Publication Data
Names: New York Times Company.
Title: Due process: defining fair legal treatment / edited by the New York Times editorial staff.
Description: New York : New York Times Educational Publishing, 2021. | Series: In the headlines | Includes glossary and index.
Identifiers: ISBN 9781642823219 (library bound) | ISBN 9781642823202 (pbk.) | ISBN 9781642823226 (ebook)
Subjects: LCSH: United States. Constitution. 5th Amendment—Juvenile literature. | United States. Constitution. 14th Amendment—Juvenile literature. | Due process of law—United States—Juvenile literature. | Civil rights—United States—Juvenile literature.
Classification: LCC KF4765.D847 2020 | DDC 347.73'5—dc23

Manufactured in the United States of America

On the cover: The U.S. Supreme Court building in Washington, D.C.; Andrew Harrer/Bloomberg Creative Photos/Getty Images.

Contents

Introduction

CONSIDERED ONE OF the fundamental guarantees of individual rights in the U.S. Constitution, due process has evolved over the course of American history. It refers to a broad range of legal proceedings meant to protect the rights of individuals. The Fifth Amendment states, in part, that "No person shall ... be deprived of life, liberty, or property, without due process of law." Similar phrasing appears again in the Constitution in the 14th Amendment, which states, in part, "nor shall any state deprive any person of life, liberty, or property, without due process of law." The reference to "any state" could arguably be interpreted to mean that states were now subject to the same limitations as the federal government — in other words, that states could not restrict individual rights in the Bill of Rights, such as an accused person's right to a speedy trial by jury. However, for decades after the 14th Amendment's ratification in 1868, the Supreme Court continued to rule that the Bill of Rights applied only to the federal government.

Freedom of speech and freedom of the press (from the First Amendment) were the first protections from the Bill of Rights to be applied to the states, in a 1925 Supreme Court case. Over the next few decades, the Court slowly began to expand this incorporation of the Bill of Rights via the 14th Amendment's due process guarantee. Many of these cases involved the rights of criminals to due process proceedings: Gideon v. Wainwright (1963) guaranteed a defendant's right to an attorney, while Miranda v. Arizona (1966) protected a person's right to remain silent after being arrested, introducing the now-well-known concept of "Miranda rights." In February 2019, the Court ruled that the Eighth Amendment's protection against excessive fines applied to the states, one of the few criminal-trial protections that had not yet been incorporated.

LIBRARY OF CONGRESS PRINTS AND PHOTOGRAPHS DIVISION

Courts at every level of jurisdiction in the United States hear cases related to due process. A U.S. district court, like this one in Cedar Rapids, Iowa, is the lowest level of federal court. Cases from it may be appealed to the circuit court and, occasionally, up to the Supreme Court.

In addition to a person's rights in civil and criminal legal proceedings, due process is also invoked in regard to the constitutionality of economic or social welfare legislation. In the early 20th century, courts routinely struck down economic regulations such as a minimum wage or a maximum number of hours that can be worked. The rationale was that such regulations restricted a person's freedom of contract, which would fall under the category of "liberty" — one of the fundamental rights that could not be abridged without due process of law under the Fifth Amendment. The Supreme Court began to uphold this sort of economic legislation beginning in the late 1930s, but the concept of "liberty," this time as it related to privacy, was the basis of the landmark abortion case Roe v. Wade in 1973.

The meaning of due process, and to whom it applies, has implications for a broad range of issues that continue to confound and divide both judges and the court of public opinion. National security concerns can interfere with due process, such as in 2010 when the administration of President Barack Obama authorized the killing of Anwar al-Awlaki, a terrorist suspect who was an American citizen. Many legal experts argued that Awlaki's American citizenship entitled him to a fair trial and that killing him was thus illegal. In 2018, President Donald Trump advocated that undocumented immigrants at the U.S. border with Mexico should be deported without any kind of hearing, a position that was inconsistent with previous court rulings that stated anyone who set foot on American soil should have the right to due process. Meanwhile, beginning in the fall of 2017, the #MeToo movement sparked a wave of accusations of sexual harassment and sexual assault — and also concerns that the accused, from prominent national figures to college students, faced unfair consequences in the public eye before they were able to defend themselves in a court of law.

These conflicts demonstrate the ongoing push and pull that due process exerts on American law and society. The articles in this book trace the history of due process from the early 20th century to the present.

CHAPTER 1

Due Process in the Early 20th Century

In the early decades of the 20th century, lawyers and judges grappled with the meaning of due process in terms of both criminal procedure and economic policy. An example of the former that captured the nation's attention was the case of Leo M. Frank, accused of murdering a woman in Atlanta in 1915. He was eventually executed, despite an appeal on the grounds that his absence from the courtroom when the verdict was announced was a violation of his due process rights. On the other hand, through the late 1930s, courts routinely struck down economic regulatory laws, arguing that they restricted a person's liberty without due process of law.

Judge Parker Speaks

BY THE NEW YORK TIMES | JULY 4, 1903

The judge addresses the Georgia Bar Association on "Due Process of Law" and says the Fourteenth Amendment is better left to courts than to the president and Congress.

TALLULAH FALLS, GA., JULY 3. — The members of the Georgia State Bar Association this morning listened to an address on "Due Process of Law," by Chief Judge Alton B. Parker of the New York State Court of Appeals. In conclusion he referred to the Fourteenth Amendment as follows:

"More and more every year is due process of law invoked, by reason of its place in the Fourteenth Amendment, to challenge the action of State Governments, and the time cannot be predicted when such efforts will cease.

"It may be safely asserted that the restraining power of the Fourteenth Amendment as against the States will be exercised far more conservatively by that court of which every citizen is justly proud, than it would be were the exercise of it confided to the other departments of the National Government.

"I feel warranted in saying that valuable beyond compare as has been the service of the Supreme Court of the United States to the people, it never has been charged with a greater responsibility than that placed upon it by the adoption of the Fourteenth Amendment, a responsibility to the meeting of which its individual members have practically devoted their supreme energies, great abilities, and broad scholarship, keeping ever in mind — as appears from the many opinions written — the danger expressed by Mr. Justice Miller of so far extending the Fourteenth Amendment as to fetter and degrade the State Governments.' "

Judge Parker said in part:

"The source of the famous phrase, 'due process of law' is to be found in the English Magna Charta. The two phrases 'due process of law' and 'the law of the land' have long been treated as synonymous.

"The phrase does not appear in the original Constitution of the United States, adopted in 1787 but was first embodied into the Constitution with Article V. of the amendments to the original Constitution, proposed by Congress in 1789. The words are also found in the Constitutions of most of the States of the Union. In some of the States the words 'due process of law' are not used, the framers of the Constitution of those States having more closely followed the phraseology of Magna Charta, 'the law of the land.'

"While the phrase came to us from England it is far more potential under our system of Government than it is or ever was in England. There, it restrained the King, not Parliament. Here it operates upon every department of Federal and State Government. In this country no provision was inserted in any Constitution that in express terms conferred upon the courts the power to set aside the statute on the ground that it offended against any provision of such Constitution. The phrase, however, proved to be a limitation on legislation in 1803, when the Supreme Court of the United States, supported by an opinion of Chief Justice Marshall, declared an act of Congress which attempted to confer original Jurisdiction on the Supreme Court under the Judiciary act null and void, on the ground that it was repugnant to the provisions of the Constitution distributing original and appellate authority.

"That famous decision, asserting for the first time a principle which lies at the very foundation of our constitutional jurisprudence, was in hostility to the views of many of our famous statesmen, among them Jefferson and Hamilton.

"One of the earliest cases of which trace is found, sustaining the principle of a 'judicial veto of a legislative act,' was brought before the Supreme Court of New Jersey and argued on constitutional grounds in 1779. The decision held that an act providing that trial by jury should be by a jury of six men was unconstitutional. Later the law thus declared unconstitutional was amended by the Legislature."

Judge Parker called attention to numerous legal cases in which the principle of "due process of law" was involved and dwelt upon the fact that in 1868 the Fourteenth Amendment became a part of the Constitution of the United States, by which amendment was incorporated in the Constitution the "due process of law" provision, to be found in most of the State Constitutions; and, this time not as a restraint upon the power of the Federal Government, as in the Fifth Amendment, but as a limitation upon the power of the States.

"At no time in the history of this country," he continued, "could this amendment have been adopted prior to the so-called reconstruction period; and if it were not now a part of the Constitution, it is not probable that it could be incorporated into that instrument. It is doubtful if it would have been adopted had it been then understood to confer upon Congress the power to enforce the restrictions on State powers contained in the amendment, and upon the Supreme Court power to set aside provisions of a State Constitution or statute which in the judgment of that court abridge the privileges or immunities of citizens of the United States, deprive any person of life, liberty, or property without due process of law, or deny to any person within the jurisdiction of the State equal protection of the laws — thereby placing the essential rights of life, liberty, and property under the ultimate protection of the National Government.

"Beyond all question support was obtained for the adoption of that amendment upon the supposition that its sole purpose was to benefit the colored race, which at that time needed protection against unfriendly action in the State where they were resident. The amendment was designed to assure to the colored race the enjoyment of all the civil rights that are enjoyed by white persons.

"The great branches of State legislation which particularly affect personal liberty and property rights are police power, the power of eminent domain, the power of taxation, and legal procedure, civil and criminal.

"It is settled that property destroyed in the proper exercise of the police power of a State need not be paid for.

"The power of a State to take private property for public use on payment of just compensation is inherent in sovereignty. Nearly all the State Constitutions prohibit such taking without just compensation and the statutes provide a due and orderly procedure in the taking. Several State Constitutions place a limitation on the Legislature in this respect and the Fourteenth Amendment prohibits a State taking without 'due process of law.'

"Concerning the power of taxation aggrieved taxpayers have frequently appealed to the Supreme Court of the United States for relief against State statutes on the ground that they offend against the due process of law provision. That court, through Justice Harlan, has said: 'In order to bring taxation imposed by a State within the scope of the Fourteenth Amendment of the National Constitution, the case should be so clearly and palpably an illegal encroachment upon private rights as to leave no doubt that such taxation is really spoliation under guise of exercising the tax power.'

"The decisions of the Supreme Court show that the tendency of later years to assume that the judicial department of the Government should review and correct the errors of the legislative and executive authorities has received little support from the United States Supreme Court considering the assaults upon taxing statutes of States and the procedure thereunder."

Due Process of Law.

REVIEW | BY THE NEW YORK TIMES | OCT. 5, 1906

An examination of the rights guaranteed the citizen by the Fifth and Fourteenth Amendments to the Federal Constitution

GENERALLY SPEAKING, there is a pretty vague notion in the average citizen's mind as to what rights and privileges are secured to him by constitutional guarantees of "due process of law." Most men, we fancy, associate the phrase with the right to trial by jury or some other such palladium of the liberties of the English-speaking race. In the present volume, "Due Process of Law Under the Federal Constitution," (Northport, L. I.: Edward Thompson Company.) the extent and nature of the rights and privileges under this head are very satisfactorily set forth, primarily for the lawyer's information, but so lucidly that the layman may read the book with distinct profit, and even pleasure.

The author, Lucius Polk McGehee, Professor of Law in the University of North Carolina, has made it his business to examine the growth, definition, and extension of the conception of "due process," principally in the light of the decisions of the Supreme Court of the United States upon causes brought to the attention of that high tribunal in virtue of the powers conferred upon the Federal Government by the "due process" clauses of the Fifth and Fourteenth Amendments to the Constitution — the latter, it may be remarked, having been found exceedingly useful for extending Federal jurisdiction, in matters other than those arising out of attempted discrimination on account of "race, color, or previous condition of servitude."

In other words the specific has turned out not to be a specific. However, the Fourteenth Amendment really does little more (except for the race, color, or previous condition of servitude provision) than to confirm and specify the powers already conferred by the Fifth Amendment — powers which were already in process of extension by judicial interpretation. The sum of these powers amounts to this — that the Federal Government is charged with the duty of insuring to all persons within its jurisdiction "due process of law."

This "due process of law, as the meaning of the words has been developed in American decisions, implies," according to Prof. McGehee, "the administration of equal laws according to established rules, not violative of the fundamental principles of private right, by a competent tribunal having jurisdiction of the case, and proceeding upon notice hearing." An examination of this definition in the light of history from Magna Charta down, and particularly in the light of the decisions of the Supreme Court of the United States tends both to show the general consistency of the growth of the principle and the reasonableness of its applications and to destroy a number of ignorant lay presumptions as to specific rights secured by the general right. Inconsistencies, of course, also develop, and cases where the particular rights secured are quite nebulous as yet. But "due process" is a constantly growing and constantly changing conception.

RETURNING TO THE DEFINITION, Prof. McGehee is at pains to show, for instance, that "established rules" do not mean particular rules. The right to due process does not bar the State from prescribing new judicial and administrative forms for accomplishing a given end; provided always, that these new forms are generally consistent with the spirit of our laws and institutions, do not violate provisions of the Federal Constitution, and are "not violative of the fundamental principles of private right." The last is the ultimate test, and the one which opens the broadest field to review by the Federal courts.

Again, due process does not require that "a competent tribunal" shall be necessarily a regular court of Justice. In many cases the Legislature which passes the law which affects a private right is a competent tribunal to decide questions affecting that private right, in many other cases administrative officers are competent tribunals; provided always they proceed according to "established rules," (that is, the rules established for them) and "proceed upon notice and hearing." The nature of the notice and hearing required may, and does, differ widely in different cases. In general the form is subject to change by State legislation. Thus it appears that the State has an undoubted right to restrict the scope of trial by jury, (within certain limits) and an equally undoubted right to endow certain administrative officers with powers quasi judicial without depriving anybody concerned of due process of law.

To the lawyer, of course, all this is commonplace. He will be interested in the detailed examination of successive decisions as they serve to define the particular things allowed or not allowed as in "due process." In his second chapter Prof. McGehee distinguishes the "elements of due process" and the tests, historical and intrinsic, and especially examines the requirement of "notice and hearing." In his third chapter he examines questions of jurisdiction — an essential element of "due process" — in his fourth chapter he discusses in detail the "rights protected by due process of law" — especially vested rights. In the same chapter is the explication of procedure.

Chapter V. is occupied with persons protected by due process, as corporations, aliens, and inhabitants of acquired territory — the extent of the rights of each class. Chapter VI. relates to the paramount rights of States as affected by and affecting considerations of due process. Chapter VII. treats taxation in the same relations, Chapter VIII. eminent domain, and Chapter IX. the police power. This last is long and especially interesting, since the author (after the authority of the best commentators) treats the police power as the residual power of Government. Here must be considered legal aspects of "business affected with a public interest," as railways, and here appear the decisions as to the regulation of rates.

NOT THE LEAST TIMELY of the questions necessarily touched by Prof. McGehee is that of divorce, the Federal decisions upon which have, it appears from his examination, left the subject in a particularly inconvenient state of doubt and anomaly. Another curious matter brought to the attention of the layman is the extraordinary power conferred upon immigration officers to determine finally and without appeal (except to the Secretary of Commerce and Labor) the fact or lack of citizenship in a person entering the country and alleged to be an alien. No such serious arbitrary power seems to reside in any other administrative officer, and the reason which appears to have moved the Supreme Court to confer it (as was done specifically by adverse decision in an appeal taken, as the court said, "in error") is, as Prof. McGehee remarks, extrajudicial. This was the practical consideration that otherwise the courts would be continually clogged with such appeals.

There is much else which deserves particular comment, for the questions discussed are those which are apt at one time or another to be of immediate interest to anybody, but space forbids. The text of the book is admirably unobstructed by confusing detail. Copious foot notes supply the references and citations, there is also an alphabetical table of citations, while the index is most satisfactorily complete.

Marshall Heard in Frank's Behalf

SPECIAL TO THE NEW YORK TIMES | FEB. 26, 1915

Mob spirit and defendant's absence at verdict were presented in an appeal to the Supreme Court. The Court is plainly interested in allegations of denial of due process of law — they continue arguments today.

WASHINGTON, FEB. 25 — The Supreme Court of the United States today heard counsel for Leo M. Frank, under sentence of death for the murder of a factory girl in Atlanta in 1913, on his appeal from the denial by the Federal District Court of Georgia of his petition for a writ of habeas corpus. Louis Marshall, of counsel for Frank, got about half way through his argument today, and it is expected that argument both for Frank and for the State of Georgia will end not later than Saturday. The court's decision probably will not be handed down for some time. A considerable portion of the hearing today was taken up in reading the brief presented in Frank's behalf which already has been summarized in The New York Times.

The Supreme Court already has declined to review the case on a writ of error. In announcing its denial of the petition the court handed down no opinion setting forth its position on the various points at issue. This silence in the earlier proceeding gave added interest to questions propounded to Mr. Marshall today by the Chief Justice and several of the Associate Justices.

Mr. Marshall discussed only two points today, the right of the accused to be present throughout the trial, particularly when the verdict was rendered, and the mob spirit alleged to have been manifested many times throughout the trial by the populace within and without the courtroom. On both points he was closely questioned, particularly by Chief Justice White and Justice Pitney.

FRANK 'COERCED' BY COURT.

Mr. Marshall's statement that Judge Roan of the trial court "coerced"

LIBRARY OF CONGRESS PRINTS AND PHOTOGRAPHS DIVISION

Leo M. Frank.

Frank into being absent when the verdict was rendered was questioned by Chief Justice White. The attorney insisted, however, that the suggestion by the Judge that Frank's life and limb and those of his counsel might be in danger if they attended amounted to coercion. He argued that the right of the accused to be present could not be denied.

"We have held that a court may abolish a trial by jury, and I do not see why a State may not abolish one of the incidents to a Jury trial," interrupted Justice Pitney. "The decisions you cite refer to Federal cases."

Mr. Marshall replied that it was a question of due process of law, and that while the Fifth Amendment to the Constitution guaranteed due process in Federal cases, the guarantee of due process in State cases in the Fourteenth Amendment was the same in effect.

When the point of mob violence was taken up, Justice Holmes remarked: "I am free to confess that point is one that impresses me very much."

"This Court has said that there must be a trial before a competent tribunal," began Mr. Marshall. "A competent tribunal is one that holds the scales of justice impartially, that is not swayed by fear or favor." Here the trial was marked by prejudice and hostility. Jeers at counsel for Frank were permitted when they lost a point. The crowd almost trespassed upon the jury box, hanging over the jury box, and their whispers were heard throughout the courtroom. Applause greeted the Solicitor General when he appeared at the seat of justice, and then the Judge held a conference, in the presence of the jury, with the Chief of Policy and a commanding officer of the State Militia.

"That was a demonstration that probably has no parallel in the history of trials. Finally, the Court asked counsel to meet him in private conference, and then, upon the insistence of the Court that the prisoner might be torn from the sanctuary of the court and lynched by a mob if he was present when the verdict was returned, counsel consented to his being absent. The jury was left to return its verdict to the prosecuting officer and the mob. They knew what that meant."

Justice Pitney inquired if the State Supreme Court had not passed upon all these facts, whereupon Justice Holmes asked if Mr. Marshall did not mean that if these were the facts it did not matter if twenty courts had passed upon them. The attorney signified his acquiescence.

THE RIGHT TO BE HEARD.

Several Justices expressed surprise that the allegations of mob violence, which Mr. Marshall dwelt upon with great earnestness, were not set forth in more detail in the record of the case. The Chief Justice and Justice Pitney questioned Mr. Marshall in some detail as to whether the absence of the accused from the courtroom when the verdict was rendered was actually a denial of the right to be heard, when he had been in the courtroom throughout the prolonged trial, had taken the stand in his own defense, and had been heard at length.

"The right to be present is a constitutional right," said Mr. Marshall. "It is part of the right to be heard. It would not have been proper to let Frank flit in and out of the courtroom, make an occasional statement, and then return to jail, as if he were not a reality but a mere abstraction."

Chief Justice White interrupted to ask: "Is it your argument that in a jury trial where the accused is not present he has not been heard and the trial has been illegal and he must go free?"

"The right to be heard," said Mr. Marshall, "includes the right to be present at the final stages of the trial as well as the earlier stages."

Chief Justice White asked Mr. Marshall to point out a passage in the Federal Constitution guaranteeing that right.

"When you say 'the right to be heard' you take into account both the question and the argument," said Chief Justice White. "The question is: What is the right to be heard?"

"The question involved here is: What is the right to be heard as applicable to a criminal trial?" replied Mr. Marshall. "Unless the right to be present is a part of the right to be heard, the court might say to a defendant at any stage: 'I do not want you to be present any further.

We can proceed with this trial without you.' Certainly a Legislature cannot say a trial can go on without the presence of the accused, or that he can be present at some stages and not at other stages."

The Chief Justice questioned Mr. Marshall regarding the fact that Frank actually was heard at length, that he testified in his own behalf, and was present in the court except when the verdict was rendered. The Chief Justice seemed to take the position that the due process of law guaranteed by the Constitution did not involve all the common law practices regarding a trial by jury. He referred to the fact that in Louisiana, his native State, where the Roman civil law prevails, the common law practice does not, and that Juries give majority instead of unanimous verdicts. He asked Mr. Marshall if he thought that practice invalidated all jury verdicts in Louisiana, and Mr. Marshall replied that he did not think the common law applied there.

After Mr. Marshall had described the incidents illustrating the mob spirit that pervaded the court room, both the Chief Justice and Justice Pitney asked him if these facts were uncontested and whether they had been laid before the Supreme Court of Georgia when the trial in the lower court was sustained. Mr. Marshall replied that some of the facts had been laid before the Supreme Court of Georgia, but that the ruling on procedure prevented a full discussion of those aspects of the trial.

Justice Hughes asked if these statements of fact had not been denied, and Justice Pitney said that the record, seemed to show that the Supreme Court of Georgia had decided the questions before it simply on technical grounds. Mr. Marshall said that Frank's counsel had misapprehended the procedure in the earlier stages of the appeals, so that there was no way by which the record could disclose the facts as to mob violence.

High Court Denies Frank's Last Plea

SPECIAL TO THE NEW YORK TIMES | APRIL 20, 1915

WASHINGTON, APRIL 19. — The Supreme Court of the United States, with a bench divided seven to two, today denied the appeal for a writ of habeas corpus for Leo M. Frank, now under sentence of death in Georgia for the murder of Mary Phagan, an Atlanta factory girl.

In denying the appeal, which came up from a Federal District Court in Georgia, the high court held that Frank's absence from the court room when the verdict was rendered did not deprive him of due process of law and that it was a right he could waive and did waive inferentially. The court also held that Frank's allegations of hostile tumult in and about the court room had been rejected by competent State tribunals as untrue.

The dissenting Justices were Messers. Holmes and Hughes, with Justice Holmes presenting their joint views. They contended that Frank had made out a prima facie case of interference with the deliberations of the jury through the prevalence of mob spirit in and about the court room, which should entitle him to a review.

Justice Pitney, in the majority opinion of more than 10,000 words, concluded with the following summary:

> *His (Frank's) allegations of hostile public sentiment and disorder in and about the courtroom, improperly influencing the trial court and the jury against him, have been rejected because found untrue in point of fact upon evidence presumably justifying that finding, and which he has not produced in the present proceeding. His contention that his lawful rights were infringed because he was not permitted to be present when the jury rendered its verdict has been set aside because it was waived by his failure to raise the objection in due season when fully cognizant of the fact.*
>
> *In all of these proceedings the State, through its courts, has retained jurisdiction over him and accorded to him the fullest right and opportunity to be heard, according to established modes of procedure, and now*

holds him in custody to pay the penalty of the crime of which he has been adjudged guilty.

In our opinion, he is not shown to have been deprived of any right guaranteed to him by the Fourteenth Amendment or any other provision of the Constitution or laws of the United States. On the contrary, he has been convicted, and is now held in custody, under "due process of law" within the meaning of the Constitution. The judgment of the District Court refusing the application for a writ of habeas corpus is affirmed.

While the general opinion here is that the Supreme Court's decision today is final and that nothing but Executive clemency can save Frank from the penalty to which he has been sentenced, the point is made in some quarters that one passage in the majority opinion seems to suggest the possibility of a further appeal. This is the passage in which the Supreme Court refuses to be moved by Frank's allegations of mob rule, on the ground that the opposing evidence upon which the State appellate courts threw out the allegations had not been presented to it by Frank's counsel. The suggestion has been made that a renewed motion with this evidence included might win the Supreme Court's attention, but advices from Atlanta tonight are that Frank's counsel seem to regard the present decision as final, and are pinning their hopes on Executive clemency.

Due Process of Law.

EDITORIAL | BY THE NEW YORK TIMES | DEC. 26, 1921

THE DECISION OF Judge Thayer of Massachusetts refusing a new trial in the case of Sacco and Vanzetti reveals a Judge determined to do justice unswayed by clamor. For him nothing existed but the law and the evidence. With conscientious painstaking, he had listened to and weighed all that could be urged by skilled counsel in behalf of the convicted men. But their appeals came down to little but this — that, the jury had wrongly judged the facts. Judge Thayer, however, points out that our laws make juries the sole judges of the facts and that the courts cannot interfere except upon clear proof that there had been manifest error in the form in which the evidence had been allowed to go before the jury, or that it had been "false to its trust." For believing the latter no sufficient reason had been adduced by the lawyers for the defense. At the last moment, to be sure, they had introduced affidavits to show that certain exhibits had been improperly admitted to the jury room. While waiting with scrupulous care to look into this allegation, Judge Thayer suspends sentence; but in all other respects he decides that Sacco and Vanzetti had enjoyed the full benefit of due process of law.

Theirs was no "crime of opinion" as Anatole France has ignorantly asserted. What they were accused of was a cold-blooded murder from motives of greed. A jury found them guilty on the evidence — a jury, moreover, plainly instructed by the Judge to put aside entirely the reported anarchistic beliefs of the prisoners. These men have been given every opportunity to establish their innocence. Their only hope of a new trial lies now in a technicality of the law, and if Judge Thayer finds that it operates in their favor he will unquestionably so decide. Either way, the dignity of the courts will have been upheld and the administration of justice vindicated.

In this country, at least, that conclusion will be accepted by nearly all. Here, in fact, there has never been any extensive and inflammatory agitation on the score of the trial of Sacco and Vanzetti. The raging and the rioting have been mostly confined to foreigners in foreign lands, not informed of the facts and inflamed by misrepresentations. Something of that will doubtless continue; no matter what the final event. But for sober men, here or abroad, it will suffice to know that every precaution known to the law has been utilized in order to prevent the possibility of a miscarriage of justice.

'Due Process of Law'

LETTER | THE NEW YORK TIMES | NOV. 2, 1924

It is argued that the Supreme Court exceeds its constitutional power in nullifying some social and economic legislation.

TO THE EDITOR OF THE NEW YORK TIMES:

James M. Rosenberg in his letter published in The Times on Oct. 24 points out that out of 45,640 statutes passed by Congress only 51 have been declared to be unconstitutional by the Supreme Court of the United States.

The figures, which I believe were compiled by Warren in his History of the United States Supreme Court, do not tell the entire story. Obviously the great bulk of Congressional statutes do not involve constitutional issues. It is important to consider what type of statute was held unconstitutional in the fifty-one cases which have nullified acts of Congress. Many of them were epochal. Many of them have thwarted Congress in its effort to legislate for the amelioration of social inequalities. Many of them are based on the opinion of the particular Judges of the Supreme Court with regard to broad questions of policy and government and are not based on constitutional difficulties which might be cleared up by the amendment. And, of course, if to these fifty-one cases were added the large number of statutes of State Legislatures which were nullified by the court the number would be very imposing and would tell a much more serious story.

No one can complain against the Supreme Court in its interpretation of the common law or of the Constitution itself. The only just cause of complaint arises when the court seizes the handle of "due process of law" to raise itself into the realms of economics and sociology and to sit as a tribunal in judgment over the people of the United States in its effort to acclimate itself to new conditions as they arise.

It might be further said that the Supreme Court has not even been consistent in its interpretation of what is and what is not due process of law with regard to social and industrial legislation. If liberty of contract, if due process of law, if unconstitutional social legislation could be precisely defined a simple amendment to the Constitution would cure their defects. But that this is not the case is plain to any student of constitutional law.

One wonders why it is that an eight-hour day for women and children in Oregon is constitutional and a minimum wage law for the women and children in the District of Columbia is unconstitutional. It is difficult to understand why if the minimum wage law for women and children in the District of Columbia is unconstitutional a law in the State of New York forbidding the employment of women and children at night is constitutional. Of course, one distinguishes between a State statute and a Congressional statute, but a Congressional statute for the District of Columbia is not very unlike State statutes for the State of New York.

The real difficulty seems to be this: Neither the fathers who framed the Constitution nor who added the Fourteenth Amendment, nor the people of the United States at any time, have had clearly in mind the function of the Supreme Court with reference to social, industrial and economic questions. Perhaps the Supreme Court is right when it says that stock dividends are not income, but the question is, Is it the intention of the body politic that the Supreme Court shall have the last say on that subject? Is it fitted by organization, by training, by capacity, adequately to consider and pass upon matters of this kind? The only fair-minded answer is in the negative. And this is regardless of the merits of the proposition urged by Senator La Follette.

These questions of industrial and economic import require solution at the hands of experts in these matters. They require speedy handling. They require a decision based on facts and not on precedents. Whether child labor should be allowed in this country or not is not a question which the common law can cast any light upon. It is a question of economics and of social policy, and as such should be decided by "social" engineers and by economic experts, and not by Judges learned in the common law and trained in the rule of precedents. Whether the Minimum Wage law is a good or a bad thing for the District of Columbia cannot be said to have been decided by the framers of the Constitution or by the Fourteenth Amendment, and if the Supreme Court is allowed the last say on that subject it requires the devastating and time-consuming procedure of a constitutional amendment to permit the passage of an act which perhaps in the opinion of every well-informed economist is an important addition to our statute books.

The country has grown impatient, not with the Supreme Court, not with its important position in the government of our land, not with its hundreds of judicial decisions, but with the one fact that it has arrogated to itself the right and privilege of having the ultimate say on questions of economic and industrial policy. If that was the intention of the framers of the Constitution it was only idly expressed by them. If that was the intention of the framers of the Fourteenth Amendment they can hardly be commended for their clarity.

Whether through the proposition urged by Senator La Follette, or whether through some other and more progressive means, this question must be met and must be answered by the people of the United States.

To justify the court completely by saying that they have nullified only 51 statutes out of 45,640 seems to be throwing the smoke-screen before the facts and to ignore the serious and pivotal importance of the fifty-one statutes which had been nullified.

MAURICE FINKELSTEIN,
New York, Oct. 26, 1924.

Ohio Liquor Courts Declared Illegal

SPECIAL TO THE NEW YORK TIMES | MARCH 8, 1927

WASHINGTON, MARCH 7. — Ohio statutes under which judicial officers presiding in "liquor courts" collect fees from defendants on conviction were declared invalid today by the United States Supreme Court. The decision was unanimous.

The case was that of Ed Tumey, plaintiff in error, against the State of Ohio. The question at issue was whether the statutes, in providing for the trial by the Mayor of a village of one accused of violating the State Prohibition act, deprived the accused of due process of law and violated the Fourteenth Amendment to the Federal Constitution because of the pecuniary and other interest which these statutes gave the Mayor in the result of the trial.

Tumey was arrested and taken before Mayor Fugh of the Village of North College Hill, charged with unlawful of possession of liquor. He moved for his dismissal, alleging that the Mayor was disqualified from trying him under the Fourteenth Amendment. The Mayor denied the motion, convicted the defendant, fined him $100 and ordered that he be imprisoned until the fine and costs were paid.

The Court of Common Pleas of Hamilton County reversed the decision of the Mayor. That court in turn was reversed by the Ohio Court of Appeals, which affirmed the judgment of the Mayor. The case came here on a writ of error to the Ohio Supreme Court.

COSTS HIS COMPENSATION.

The evidence showed that Mayor Fugh acted under a village ordinance for enforcement of the State liquor law, which provided that the Mayor should retain his costs in each liquor case, in addition to his salary, as compensation for hearing the case. The record showed that between May 11 and Dec. 31, 1923, the total amount of fines and cost collected by this village court was upward of $20,000, of which the Mayor received $696.35.

"That officers acting in a judicial or quasi-judicial capacity are disqualified by their interest in the controversy to be decided is, of course, the general rule," said Chief Justice Taft in today's opinion. "It certainly violates the Fourteenth Amendment and deprives a defendant in a criminal case of due process of law to subject his liberty or property to the judgment of a court the Judge of which has a direct, personal, substantial, pecuniary interest in reaching a conclusion against him in his case. The Mayor of the Village of North College Hill, Ohio, had a direct, personal, pecuniary interest in convicting the defendant who came before him for trial, in the $12 of costs imposed in his behalf, which he would not have received if the defendant had been acquitted.

"This was not exceptional, but was the result of the normal operation of the law and the ordinance. Counsel for the State assert the validity of the practice as an exception to the general rule."

NOT SUPPORTED BY PRECEDENT.

The Chief Justice pointed out that the practice of inferior judicial officers receiving fees on condition that they convicted the defendants cannot find support as due process of law in English precedent. He said the practice "has prevailed and still prevails in Arkansas, Kentucky, Nebraska, North Carolina, Georgia, Ohio and Texas, and it seems at one time to have obtained in Indiana, Oregon, Illinois and Alabama."

"It is finally argued," said Chief Justice Taft in conclusion, "that the evidence shows clearly that the defendant was guilty and that he was only fined $100, which was the minimum amount, and therefore that he cannot complain of a lack of due process, either in his conviction or in the amount of the judgment. The plea was not guilty and he was convicted.

"No matter what the evidence was against him, he had the right to have an impartial Judge. He seasonably raised the objection and was entitled to halt the trial because of the disqualification of the Judge, which existed both because of his direct pecuniary interest in the outcome and because of his official motive to convict and to graduate the fine to help the financial needs of the village. There were thus presented at the outset both features of the disqualification."

Cleaners' Code Voided in Jersey

SPECIAL TO THE NEW YORK TIMES | MARCH 12, 1936

NEWARK, N. J., MARCH 11. — The price-fixing provisions of the New Jersey law enacted in June, 1935, to regulate the cleaning and dyeing industry were held to be in violation of the "due process" clause of the Federal Constitution in an opinion handed down today by a Statutory Federal Court of three judges here.

The court comprised Circuit Judge J. Warren Davis and District Judges William Clark and Phillip Forman. The opinion was written by Judge Clark, with the other two judges concurring. The decision said an injunction would be issued restraining David T. Wilentz, Attorney General of New Jersey, the State board of the cleaning and dyeing trade and other State officials from enforcing the act.

The suit for an injunction was brought by Consolidated Cleaners and Dyers, Inc., and its affiliated Kent Stores of New Jersey, which operate a plant in Hillside and a chain of twenty-six retail stores in the northern part of the State. Later similar suits were filed by the Federal Cleaners and Dyers, Inc., operators of twelve North Jersey stores, and Re-Nu-It, operator of two Newark stores.

EMERGENCY IS NO EXCUSE

The court held that the Legislature's declaration of an emergency in the act did not validate it. The court held also that the cleaning and dyeing industry "is not a business affected with a public interest and is immune, therefore, from legislative price fixing," and that regulation of the industry under the law was not a "reasonable exertion of governmental authority."

The court said that the unfair trade preventions and sanitary regulations in the act were constitutional, but were features of the plan of which price fixing was a part, and that the price-fixing provision was not considered separable.

Isadore H. Colton, a member of counsel to the cleaning and dyeing board, said the decision would be appealed. The appeal will be directly to the United States Supreme Court under the law, he said. He added that at the hearing on the terms of the injunction, which probably would be next week, the court would be asked "to consider the advisability of omitting therefrom the unfair competition, hours of labor and sanitary regulations, which it intimated itself to be constitutional."

The opinion suggested the possibility of handling "predatory price cutting both as a common law tort and as a method of unfair competition."

GROUP FORMED, PRICES SET

Joseph Feldheim, president of Consolidated and of Kent Stores, announced that at a meeting this evening in his Hillside plant an organization of chain cleaners had been formed to prevent a price war. The group will be known as the Chain Cleaners Association, with Mr. Feldheim as president. He said all the chain operators in the State, numbering sixteen, and doing 60 per cent of the business in the State, had joined the association and had set a temporary price of 49 cents, effective Saturday, for cleaning a suit. The minimum set by the outlawed board was 59 cents.

Mr. Feldheim said his own chain would return between $12,000 and $15,000 in service to customers as the result of the decision. He said that his price before Dec. 20 was 29 cents for cleaning a suit, and since that date the customer had received a rebate slip for the difference between the board's minimum and the former price, to be made good in trade if the minimum was voided. The minimum was set by the board on Dec. 20.

The State dyers' code was adopted last Spring by the Legislature to take the place of the invalidated Federal dyers' code, which was part of the NRA. Some of the cleaners and dyers were enthusiastic about a State code, while others attacked it as merely a vehicle for more political patronage.

CHAPTER 2

Due Process Evolves in the 1930s and 1940s

In the late 1930s, the Supreme Court began to loosen its interpretation of due process in relation to economic regulations. For example, in a reversal of a 1923 decision, a case in 1938 ruled that states could set a minimum wage for employees. While most protections for defendants were only guaranteed in federal courts during this era, some legal scholars and observers were beginning to argue in favor of extending those due process rights to state cases. Critics of the Red Scare contended that suspected Communists were denied due process and fair trials.

'Due Process' Made an Issue

BY LEWIS WOOD | MARCH 7, 1937

The phrase used in two Amendments to the Constitution has a strange history.

WASHINGTON, MARCH 6. — When in a Washington Summer seventy-one years ago the Fourteenth Amendment to the Constitution was written by Congress there was not the remotest public suggestions that the "due-process" clause would be used some day to protect private business against State laws.

The Fourteenth Amendment was forged in the flaming passions of Reconstruction days. As the Reconstructionists strode across the

Congressional stage they indicated that in lifting the "due-process" clause from the Fifth Amendment and welding it into the Fourteenth they intended solely to defend the newly acquired rights of freed slaves.

Worn old volumes of The Congressional Globe demonstrate the point recently reiterated by Senator Borah and other lawyers seeking to resolve the Supreme Court controversy through a constitutional change preventing the high justices from condemning State law through use of the due-process wording.

Thaddeus Stevens, hard-bitten Pennsylvanian, shouted to the House that "whatever law protects the white man shall afford equal protection to the black; whatever means of redress is afford to one shall be afforded to all." James A. Garfield, future President, emphasized the "proposal to hold over every American citizen, without regard to color, the protecting shield of law."

DISCUSSION BRIEF

There was very little discussion of the due-process clause during the month and a half the amendment was passing through Congress. Every one seemed to accept it without controversy. Imbedded in the first section of the amendment, the language was hurriedly disposed of so that fire might be concentrated upon the other, more specific, sections.

The amendment finally went through in a period of exquisite tension and ranging antagonisms. Born in the Joint Committee on Reconstruction, it was reported to the House by Mr. Stevens on April 30, 1866, debated May 8-10 and adopted by a vote of 128 to 37. Two weeks later Senate debate started and continued until June 8, when the plan was approved 33 to 11.

"Grave doubts" of the amendment's constitutionality impelled Andrew Johnson to send a message to Congress, but he formally permitted Secretary Seward to present the constitutional change for State ratification, which was accomplished on July 28, 1868.

Buried in the amendment, the due-process clause attracted little attention for years. Its presence there apparently clothed it with no new significance. In the Fifth Amendment, as a part of the Bill of Rights, it had been generally regarded as an assurance that the government could not invade the basic privileges of the citizen. In the Fourteenth it was looked upon merely as a barrier against State intrusion upon these guarantees.

While, historians say, attorneys sought to make use of the due-process clause in behalf of an individual as early as the Dred Scott case, it was only after the passage of the Fourteenth Amendment that it came frequently to be employed by corporations against State legislation. In these latter days courts have been asked innumerable times to protect private enterprise against deprivation of liberty and property "without due process of law."

Endless controversies have occurred over the due-process clause. Today the legal procession entertains varying ideas about it. The phrasing is, as Chief Justice Hughes once said, "vague." But the Supreme Court evidently maintains that so long as the language remains unqualified it is susceptible of use in a legal attack.

VIEWS OF HUGHES

In 1928, when Mr. Hughes had retired as associate justice and before he returned as Chief Justice, he outlined the court's attitude toward the existence of this language in the Constitution.

"When in the year of grace 1866," he said, "there is placed in the Constitution of the United States a declaration that no State shall deprive any person of life, liberty or property without due process of law, can a State make anything due process of law which, by its own legislation, it chooses to declare as such?

"To affirm this is to hold that the prohibition to the State is of no avail, or has no application where the invasion of private rights is effected under the forms of State legislation."

Supreme Court Clears Away Old Tangles

BY DEAN DINWOODEY | APRIL 4, 1937

Mr. Dinwoodey is the editor of United States Law Week.

WASHINGTON, APRIL 3. — The significance of last Monday's decisions of the Supreme Court, particularly that in the minimum-wage case, it is already being recognized extends beyond their immediate important results and their timely relation to the present controversy over the court and its past decisions.

There is seldom a more dramatic occurrence in the Supreme Court than the disavowal of a prior ruling on an important constitutional issue. And last Monday the court turned its back, after a period of fourteen years, on one of its most widely criticized decisions.

In the circumstances, also, it was inevitable that any decision of the court on a vital constitutional point would be seized upon both to support and to oppose the pending plan for increase in membership of the court. That there was closely divided vote in the one case offered another reason for an exchange of arguments. But it may be expected that the constitutional implications of the three major decisions of last week will overshadow any political considerations ascribed to them.

The larger importance of the decisions lies in the renewed indication of a disposition of the court not to interpose constitutional objections to freedom of action by the States and by the Federal Government in their well-recognized spheres of constitutional authority; in other words, not to hold in conflict with the Constitution, unless clearly arbitrary, statutes enacted by the State and Federal Governments, provided the subject-matter of the legislation is that over which either, as the case may be, has clear authority.

THREE MAJOR RULINGS

This disposition of the court translated into decisions, is evidenced by the rulings last Monday in three major cases:

(1) That the States, in the exercise of their police power, may fix minimum wages for women and children;

(2) That Congress, in the exercise of its commerce power, may require collective bargaining with employees by employers engaged in interstate rail transportation; and

(3) That Congress, in the exercise of its bankruptcy power, may authorize the stay of foreclosure of farm properties and modify the rights of mortgage holders.

There was no question as to the sphere of constitutional authority of the State in the minimum-wage case, or of the Federal Government in the bankruptcy case, over the subject-matter of the statutes involved in the cases; no question as to which, if either, had constitutional authority in the particular field of the legislation. This issue, though raised and considered, was a secondary one in the Railway Labor Act case.

The decisions thus did not deal with the division of authority between the Federal and State governments embodied in the constitutional doctrine of dual sovereignty. Therefore, the ruling that a State has constitutional power to prescribe minimum wages lends no support to the contention that the Federal Government has a similar constitutional power. Nor can the argument that the Federal Government has authority to require collective bargaining in manufacturing industries be directly supported by the decision that it has such authority in the case of interstate rail carriers. The latter problem may be decided by the court in the Wagner act cases, and the decisions therein may shed some light as to a possible determination of the first problem. The Supreme Court several years ago decided that a State may, in certain circumstances, provide a moratorium on property foreclosures.

THE DUE-PROCESS CLAUSE

The decisions in the three cases, in which no constitutional objections were found to the particular exercises of the police power by the State of Washington, and of the commerce and bankruptcy power by Congress, arose from a more liberal interpretation of the due-process clause of the Constitution. This clause, first included in the Fifth Amendment and repeated in the Fourteenth Amendment, provides that neither the Federal nor State Government shall deprive any person "of life, liberty or property without due process of law." The major contention in each case was that this constitutional guarantee was infringed.

The more liberal interpretation placed by the Supreme Court on the due-process clause is best illustrated, perhaps, by the decision in the minimum-wage case, in which four justices dissented. The court has heretofore held that the "liberty" spoken of in the due-process clause includes "freedom of contract." And it was upon this conception that the District of Columbia law permitting the fixing of minimum wages was held by a five-to-three vote to violate the due-process clause, on the ground that it was an unreasonable restraint of freedom of contract.

Now, however, while the conception of "freedom of contract" as a component of "liberty" still persists, the five-man majority on the court has ruled that minimum-wage laws do not arbitrarily strain "liberty," in the sense that the Supreme Court now interprets the meaning of that word. The liberality of interpretation is made clearer by declarations of Chief Justice Hughes in his opinion than by a statement of the result of that decision. Mr. Hughes said:

> *The Constitution does not speak of freedom of contract. It speaks of liberty and prohibits the deprivation of liberty without due process of law. In prohibiting that deprivation the Constitution does not recognize an absolute and uncontrollable liberty. Liberty in each of its phrases has its history or connotation.*
>
> *But liberty safeguarded in a social organization which requires the protection of law against the evils which menace the health, safety, morals and welfare of the people. Liberty under the Constitution is thus necessarily subject to the restraints of due process, and regulation which*

is reasonable in relation to its subject and is adopted in the interest of the community is due process.

These declarations of the Chief Justice are considered by some of those familiar with the course of the court's decisions to state a broad view of the police power of the States which encompasses not only the authority to fix minimum wages for women and children but also for men and to legislate along other lines of social welfare.

THE ADKINS DECISION

The Adkins decision of 1923, holding invalid the law of Congress fixing minimum wages for women in the District of Columbia, and the Morehead ruling of last June, affirming a decision holding the New York wage law unconstitutional, both severely criticized decisions, were obstacles to the free exercise of the police power. Not only did the Adkins decisions forestall wage regulation, but upon the authority of that decision other regulatory legislation was voided.

The action of the court last Monday in overruling the Adkins case and substituting in its place the decision in the Washington case, when considered with the Nebbia decision of 1934, in which the power of the States to fix prices was broadly sustained also by the five justices who validated the Minimum Wage Law, may mean that the Supreme Court, so long as the current majority continues, will find that the Constitution is not infringed by any State statute fixing wages or prices which has a reasonable relation to a proper legislative purpose and is neither arbitrary nor discriminatory.

A number of unusual circumstances have attended litigation over the validity of State minimum-wage laws. Some of them are:

The Supreme Court has rendered five minimum-wage decisions. In all five instances, despite the contrariety of decision, the judgments of the lower courts were affirmed.

A numerical count of individuals who have voted on the constitutionality of such laws would show, even before last week's decision, that a majority of them voted to uphold laws prescribing minimum wages.

This anomaly results from the fact that there was more frequent change in the personnel of the favorable group than in that unfavorable.

VOTE ON OREGON LAW

The first case, involving an Oregon law, similar to the Washington statute, was sustained by a four-to-four vote of the Supreme Court. Justice Brandeis did not participate because of a connection with the case before he was appointed a member of the court. But for this circumstance the whole course of minimum-wage legislation might have been different.

And the Supreme Court of Washington on three separate occasions sustained the validity of the Washington law. The two earlier cases were not carried to the Supreme Court of the United States.

The three major decisions of last Monday, taken with other decisions of the same justices during the last three years, may be said to show certain tendencies of the decision of the present court:

(1) To restrict the enactments and activities of the Federal Government to those matters which are clearly within the powers granted to it by the Constitution, as, in the case of the commerce clause, for example, to restrict the Federal Government to the regulation and promotion of commerce which is unmistakably interstate, and to leave the rest to the States.

(2) To raise no constitutional object to free exercise of Federal and State powers within the respective constitutional spheres of government.

ISSUES NARROWED DOWN

It may be considered, after Monday's rulings and the wiping out of the "no-man's land" that had existed, that the last stated tendency has become quite definite. Less definite is the first stated tendency. The awaited rulings in the Wagner act cases will make more certain the view of the court as to the extent of the Federal Government's commerce power. The court's recent decisions have served, at least, to narrow and emphasize the issues between the Executive and the judiciary.

High Court Silent on Search Rights

BY DEAN DINWOODEY | JULY 3, 1938

WASHINGTON, JULY 2. — Now the New York Constitutional Convention has decided, subject to final action, to place before the electorate, the question whether New York's Constitution shall contain a prohibition against unreasonable search and seizure, the issue may be raised of the need of any such provision in the State's fundamental law.

This issue, if it arises during public debate on the proposed constitutional change, will probably revolve about the problem of whether the Federal Constitution adequately safeguards the citizen against reasonable search and seizure, and so makes unnecessary any duplicating prohibition in the State Constitution.

A specific prohibition in the Federal Constitution against unreasonable searches and seizures appears in the Fourth Amendment, which reads as follows:

> *The right of the people to be secure in their persons, houses, papers and effects, against reasonable searches and seizures shall not be violated, and no warrants shall issue but upon probable cause, supported by oath or affirmation, and particularly describing the place to be searched and the persons or things to seized.*

DUE-PROCESS CLAUSE

But this amendment, like other initial amendments, which contain the Bill of Rights, constitutes restrictions on the Federal Government, not on the State Governments. The history of adoption of the first eight amendments makes this plain, and it has been so declared many times by the Supreme Court.

It is not the Fourth Amendment, but rather the Fourteenth, containing the due-process clause, to which any opponents of the recommended addition of a search-and-seizure provision to the New York

Constitution may point. The clause reads:

> *No State shall make or enforce any law which shall abridge the privileges or immunities of citizens of the United States, nor shall any State deprive any person of life, liberty or property without due process of law, nor deny to any person within its jurisdiction the equal protection of the laws.*

It may be contended that this clause prohibits any unreasonable search or seizure by State and municipal enforcement officials, and so renders unneeded any similar proscription in the New York State charter.

COURT DECISIONS

Decisions of the Supreme Court of the United States construing the due-process clause lend some substance to such a claim. Twenty years ago the argument that the Fourteenth Amendment covers searches and seizures, subjects not mentioned therein, would have been deemed not well taken; but by reason of decisions of the Supreme Court during the past several years it may now be considered that the argument has acquired some plausibility.

The court has decided that some of the fundamental personal rights and liberties of a citizen are protected by the due-process clause from impairment by the States. The court has said that such protection comes, not by virtue of the fact that that those personal rights are enumerated in the first eight amendments, "but because they are of such a nature that they are included in the conception of due process of law."

This construction of the Fourteenth Amendment to embrace the protection of civil rights began in 1925, when the Supreme Court said that freedom of speech and of the press was protected by the due-process clause against action by States.

REAFFIRMATION IN MARCH

The court reaffirmed this constitutional rule last March in a decision holding a handbill ordinance unconstitutional. It stated that

> *freedom of speech and freedom of the press, which are protected by the First Amendment from infringement by Congress, are among the fundamental personal rights and liberties which are protected by the Fourteenth Amendment from invasion by State action.*

Since the first of such decisions in 1925, the court by other decisions has declared that the right of peaceable assembly, the right of free exercise of religion and the right of one accused of crime to the benefit of counsel, come under the protective arm of the Fourteenth Amendment. State statutes and State action invading these rights, together with those of freedom of speech and freedom of press, have been held to violate the due-process clause.

Difficulty will be experienced in relating these recent decisions to earlier ones. In an earlier decision, the high court had asserted that

> *neither the Fourteenth Amendment nor any other provision of the Constitution of the United States imposes upon the States any restriction about "freedom of speech" or the "liberty of silence"; nor, we may add, does it confer any right of privacy upon either persons or corporations.*

'LIBERTY' STRESSED

It is the word "liberty" in the text which has been used as a vehicle by the court for its recent decisions bringing certain civil rights within the protection of the due-process clause.

Whether the right against unreasonable search and seizure is among the civil rights — "the fundamental personal rights and liberties" — which are protected by the Fourteenth Amendment from impairment by State and municipal governments and their officers still remains to be determined. That it may not be so considered by the Supreme Court is evidenced by a decision of the tribunal which was written several months ago by Associate Justice Cardozo.

He rejected the argument that whatever would be a violation of the original Bill of Rights contained in the first eight amendments to the Federal Constitution, if done by the Federal Government, would be equally unlawful by force of the Fourteenth Amendment if done by a State. The right to trial by jury and the right of immunity from prosecution except as the result of an indictment, he declared, are not among those civil rights safeguarded by the Fourteenth Amendment; and he indicated that, in his opinion, neither is the right against unreasonable search or seizure so safeguarded.

Due Process

EDITORIAL | BY THE NEW YORK TIMES | MARCH 12, 1940

FOR THE SECOND TIME in a month the Supreme Court has reversed the conviction of a Negro on the ground that his confession had been illegally obtained. Reference was made in the decision, which this time was not accompanied by a formal opinion, to the opinion delivered by Justice Black in the case of four Florida Negroes on Feb. 12. It is worth while to recall one or two fine passages in the Feb. 12 opinion. After pointing out that the Florida prisoners had not confessed until they had been exposed to a week of almost continuous "grilling," Justice Black went on to say:

> *To permit human lives to be forfeited upon confessions thus obtained would make of the constitutional requirement of due process of law a meaningless symbol. ... Due process of law ... commands that no such practice as that disclosed by this record shall send any accused to his death. No higher duty, no more solemn responsibility, rests upon this court than that of translating into living law and maintaining this constitutional shield deliberately planned and inscribed for the benefit of every human being subject to our Constitution — of whatever race, creed or persuasion.*

The implications of these two decisions are not limited to the Southern States or to the Negro race. They cover the use of the third degree, or violence or threats by any officer of the law in any State against any prisoner. In protecting the "poor, the ignorant, the numerically weak, the friendless and the powerless" (to quote again from the Feb. 12 opinion), the high court stands on guard with flaming sword over the rights of every one of us.

Ouster of 4 Reds by Union Upheld

BY THE NEW YORK TIMES | APRIL 22, 1947

Justice Hammer rejects the plea that men were deprived of due process by ILGWU.

IN A DECISION hailed by union counsel as a "milestone in the defense of American labor against Communist deceit and treachery," Supreme Court Justice Ernest E. L. Hammer upheld yesterday the suspension of four leaders of a Communist faction from membership in the International Ladies Garment Workers Union, AFL.

The four men — Arnold Ames, Charles Nemeroff, Irving Kotler and Emanuel Brownstein — were suspended from the Cutters Union, Local 10 of the ILGWU, for periods of three to five years on charges of circulating defamatory literature against David Dubinsky, president, and other officers of the garment union. The suspensions were ordered after a union trial in July, 1944, and the suspended men have been depicted as "martyrs" in the Communist press ever since.

In a forty-page decision, Justice Hammer rejected charges that they had been deprived of due process or had not had a fair and impartial hearing. He cited at length from the writings of Nicolai Lenin, Joseph Stalin and William Z. Foster, national chairman of the Communist party, to prove that Communists were under standing instructions to use fraud, deceit and trickery whenever it might serve the party's purposes.

Excoriating the arguments put forward by the accused men as "an exhibition of communistic double-talk," Justice Hammer said:

"On the one hand are seen irresponsible defamatory statements attacking leaders of high standing among union workers and their fellow-American citizens as well, couched in provocative phrases overloaded with adjectives of insinuation and invective calculated through deceit to ruin their reputations with their fellow-unionists.

"On the other hand, acts praiseworthy as American citizens are held up for scorn and ridicule as being anti-Soviet, and associations of interest and value to union workers are seized upon to suggest, and thereby to stir up, race prejudice."

Emil Schlesinger, attorney for the ILGWU, said the decision demonstrated the determination of the courts to prevent totalitarian forces from using democratic institutions as a weapon in their efforts to overthrow democracy. He expressed certainty that the ruling would serve as a precedent in future cases affecting Communist penetration of trade unions.

Due Process in Washington

EDITORIAL | BY THE NEW YORK TIMES | AUG. 4, 1948

IF THERE IS ONE THING above all others in our American way of life in which most thoughtful citizens take pride and in which they firmly believe, it is in the principles of civil rights enunciated in the first ten amendments to our Constitution. They were attached to the Constitution on the demand of the people of the thirteen colonies before they would accept the Constitution itself. They make up what is popularly called our Bill of Rights. Among these are a guarantee against being called to answer for an infamous crime except upon Grand Jury indictment, a promise of open trial by a jury of one's peers, the right to confront one's accusers in open court after having been previously informed of the nature and the cause of the accusations. We do not believe these fundamental rights are being observed today in Washington by the Congressional Committees investigating communism in the United States. Let us look at the record.

Two former high officials of the Government, and others, have been accused by Miss Elizabeth T. Bentley, herself a confessed former spy for the Communists, with having engaged in espionage during the war, with having violated their oaths of office, with having acted as unregistered agents of a foreign government. Did they learn of these charges of commission of infamous crimes through official channels, or on being called to answer an indictment? They did not. At least one first learned of Miss Bentley's testimony through a call from a newspaper reporter. They already had been broadcast to the world. How substantial are these charges?

Before appearing before the House Committee on Un-American Activities Miss Bentley testified before a Federal Grand Jury in New York City that was investigating wartime espionage activities. Presumably she gave the same testimony there that she did in Washington. Did the Grand Jury indict the men against whom she made the charges? It did not. Before appearing before the House Committee Miss Bentley also gave the same testimony before an executive session of the Senate sub-committee headed by Senator Ferguson that is conducting a parallel inquiry. Did they make public her testimony or allow her to give it in open hearing? They did not. Yet a day later Chairman Thomas of the House Committee calls her to the witness stand and lets her make the charges openly.

To grant Mr. Remington, Mr. Currie, Mr. White and others named by Miss Bentley an opportunity later to confront her in the Committee room and answer her charges does not rectify the basic wrong that has been done. Many will read, and perhaps believe, the charges but not the rebuttal. There is even no guarantee that these accused will ever have their day in court. Dr. Edward U. Condon was accused a year ago by the Thomas Committee of being "the weakest link in our atomic energy set-up" and he has yet to be given an opportunity to answer before the Committee.

There undoubtedly were, and still are, agents of the Soviet Government, and of other governments, in this country seeking information on military matters that is not available to them through official channels. They should be sought out, brought to trial and punished, if they are found guilty. There are legal ways of doing that, such as the Royal Commission used in Canada in investigating the leakage of information on atomic research. It conducted its hearings in private, weighed the evidence and only then made public the charges.

We have a precious heritage in this country of protection of the innocent against false accusation, of a fair trial even for the guilty. What price a few headlines if those rights are compromised or violated? A dubious security purchased by those means would be bought far too high.

Police vs. Due Process

REVIEW | BY HENRY STEELE COMMAGER | JAN. 16, 1949

LIBERTY AGAINST GOVERNMENT:
The Rise, Flowering, and Decline of a Famous Juridical Concept
By Edward S. Corwin. 210 pp.
Baton Rouge, La.: Louisiana State University Press. $3.

ONE OF THE PARADOXES of American history is that the first democracy should also be the first country to establish elaborate constitutional barriers against democracy. Faith in people and fear of government are twin inheritances of the Revolution, parallel doctrines of some of the Founding Fathers. Jefferson, who most eloquently set forth both principles — the principle that government originates with men and the principle that that government is best which governs least — was untroubled by the paradox.

Later generations have not been so fortunate.

In a sense this is the central problem of American constitutional history. Constitutionally it can be put (somewhat too glibly) in *terras* of broad versus narrow construction; legally it can be put in terms of the conflict between the police power and the due process clause. It is this problem with which Dr. Corwin, Emeritus Professor of Jurisprudence at Princeton, is concerned.

Fear of government is easy to explain. History and experience, as Dr. Corwin indicates, had taught the Founding Fathers that all government tended toward tyranny and that the highest achievement of statesmanship was the fabrication of safeguards against the pretensions and usurpations of government. "Government, like dress," said Tom Paine, "is the badge of lost innocence." And old John Adams, who was no friend of Paine, rejoiced that he had written some thirteen different checks and balances into the Constitution of Massachusetts.

What is more difficult to explain is how it happened that fear of government persisted, even into an era of democracy. It was partly, to be sure, what John Jay said, that "it takes time to make subjects into citizens," but it was more complicated than that. By the mid-twentieth century that transformation has been completed, but fear of government persists, and has, indeed, been elevated into a political principle by one of the major political parties.

The explanation, Dr. Corwin suggests, is to be found in the fact that the concept of liberty came to be identified with that of property. Elements dominant in politics generally at the beginning of our history and powerful in legal and political circles throughout, came to fear that property rights were endangered by democracy. That government had been originally designed to protect men in their life, liberty and property had been explained by Locke and accepted by the Revolutionary Fathers. That a government under popular control would inevitably threaten property as well as liberty seemed clear.

It was necessary, therefore, to find or devise legal and constitutional principles which would restrain government from attacking property as well as liberty. The easiest way to do this was to identify the two, to write limitations on government into the Constitution, and to entrust to the judiciary the task of maintaining those limitations.

THE PRINCIPLE THAT government was limited had a long and respectable lineage, and so, too, the parallel principle that governmental action beyond certain fixed limits was null and void. But what were those limits — and who was to define them? Some, to be sure, were written into the constitutional documents, state and Federal. But these were at once inadequate and vague.

It was all very well, Dr. Corwin points out, to provide that no state should impair the obligation of a contract, but what was the obligation of a contract, and who was to decide when such an obligation had been impaired? It was all very well to guarantee that no person should be deprived of property without "due process of law." But what was "due process of law," and of what value was the guarantee when it did not apply to the states — inevitably the chief offenders against property rights?

Something more was necessary, and something more was fabricated. What emerged was what Dr. Corwin calls the doctrine of vested rights — a doctrine that was largely a judicial creation. What this doctrine meant was, simply, that government could not deprive any person of property already acquired. Or, in the author's words,

> *that the effect of legislation on existing property rights was a primary test of its validity, for if these were essentially impaired then some clear constitutional justification must be found for the legislation or it must succumb to judicial condemnation.*

THIS NOTION EMERGED, first, in Chase's opinion in Clader v. Bull, and received official sanction, as it were, in Marshall's remarkable opinion in Fletcher v. Peck — an opinion which skillfully incorporated "natural law" into the Constitution. The gains that Marshall won for property, Story consolidated, first in his opinions and later in his "Commentaries on the Constitution."

Gradually the doctrine of vested rights took on formidable proportions. Eminent domain was whittled away; the tax power was cramped and limited; the police power was regarded with suspicion. "Every statute," said Story, "which takes away or impairs vested rights acquired under existing laws, or creates a new obligation, imposes a new duty, or attaches a new disability in respect to transactions or considerations already past, must be deemed retrospective," and therefore void.

With the notorious Dred Scott decision this doctrine was fully established in constitutional law. For in the long run the most important part of that decision was the argument that the prohibition of slavery in the Territories was a deprivation of the right of holding property, without due process of law.

THE STORY IS too familiar to justify rehearsal. What it all amounted to, as Dr. Corwin neatly remarks, was the elimination of "due process" from the due process clause, making that clause read, merely, that "no state shall deprive any person of life, liberty or property."

There were, to be sure, protesting voices, even from the bench. More effective than an attack upon the interpretation of due process was the development of the full potentialities of the "police power." From the Eighteen Eighties on, "police power" waged war with "due process" — with the courts as partisan arbiters. Not until Holmes and Brandeis came on the United States Supreme Court was there effective protest against the misuse of due process to bar necessary governmental action. Not until the New Deal and the "court-packing" threat was that meaning finally abandoned.

With its abandonment came a new appreciation of the importance of the term "liberty," a new emphasis on the Fourteenth Amendment as a protection for civil rights and equality. That long and impressive series of cases that began with the Gitlow Case and has continued to this day has not only largely repudiated the old restrictive concept of the term "due process" but has made it a positive instrument for the protection of personal liberties.

Thus the Court is taking us back to the intention of the framers of the Fourteenth Amendment — back, perhaps, to the intention of the Framers of the Constitution.

Mr. Corwin is the most learned of all our commentators on constitutional history, and the most perspicacious. He has here dealt with a significant chapter of that history with his customary lucidity and learning. To historians one of the chief values of this little book will be its recapitulation of the long history of the concept of natural law limitations on government. To lawyers it will reveal the dangers that flow from the perversion of constitutional principles to class purposes. To laymen it may well demonstrate that, with a mature people, sound doctrine triumphs in the end over unsound.

The author has been a severe critic of the Old Court that, unwept and unsung, ended its long reign in 1937. It would be an exaggeration to say that he has been an uncritical champion of the New Court that has staggered, from decision to decision, back to the great tradition of American constitutionalism. He ends his book with a statement of possibilities, rather than a prophecy, posed first by Tocqueville and as yet not fully resolved:

> *The nations of our time cannot prevent the conditions of men from becoming equal; but it depends upon themselves whether the principle of equality is to lead them to servitude or freedom, to knowledge or barbarism, to prosperity or to wretchedness.*

A Professor of History at Columbia University, **DR. COMMAGER** is the author of "America in Perspective" and other books on American history and government.

CHAPTER 3

Expansion of Due Process During the Civil Rights Movement

During the civil rights movement, due process was cited in decisions such as the integration of schools in Little Rock, Ark., and James Meredith's enrollment as the first black student at the University of Mississippi. Under Chief Justice Earl Warren (1953–69), the Supreme Court vastly expanded the scope of due process in a series of cases that granted the trial protections of the Bill of Rights to criminal defendants in state cases.

Civil Rights Gain in 1955 Described

BY THE NEW YORK TIMES | JAN. 23, 1956

CIVIL RIGHTS MADE strong gains in 1955, but "a terrifying lot of unfinished business" remains, the American Civil Liberties Union said in its annual report yesterday.

The report listed the key development of the year as the Federal court defense of due process and equal treatment under the law.

It cited judicial decisions limiting the State Department's power to deny passports to citizens and "continuing to break through barriers of discrimination and segregation in education and places of public accommodation."

Patrick Murphy Malin, executive director of the A. C. L. U., wrote in the report that "our high courts and principal executive agencies are continuing to do a good job in clearing the main channel of equality before the law."

CITES NEGRO COERCION

"The Interstate Commerce Commission has ordered that racial segregation on interstate trains and buses, and in station waiting rooms serving their passengers, must end," he noted.

"But a terrifying lot of unfinished business will face us for a long time to come. Emmett Till is kidnapped and killed in Mississippi, neo-Klan organizations exert various kinds of coercion on Negroes in many parts of the South, and in the North, whose holier-than-thou bluff is being called by the rapid increase of its Negro population, discrimination in public housing takes on alarming proportions.

"Nor do we have all the time in the world to attend to this unfinished business. Africa and Arabia and Asia are looking ever more closely at us, and they hate to see much of what they see."

In a section devoted to "Equality Before the Law," the report declared:

"The United States Supreme Court has spoken twice. The Executive Branch of the Government has acted with general success in the integration of the armed forces, and with great success in the sphere of Government contracts. But Congress, as has been pointed out by the National Association for the Advancement of Colored People, has done nothing."

"The A. C. L. U. and others will ... continue to press for changes in the Federal civil rights laws which will enable the Federal Government to take more direct action in protection of minority group rights."

High Court Bars Death for Negro

SPECIAL TO THE NEW YORK TIMES | JAN. 15, 1957

WASHINGTON, JAN. 14 — The Supreme Court set aside today the death sentence imposed by an Alabama Court on William Earl Fikes, a Negro, who was convicted of burglary with intent to commit rape.

The Supreme Court ruled, 6 to 3, that two confessions made by Fikes had been obtained by procedures that violated due process of law. The Fifth and Fourteenth Amendments to the Constitution say that no person shall be deprived of life, liberty or property without due process.

Chief Justice Earl Warren wrote the major opinion. He was joined by Justices Hugo L. Black, William O. Douglas and Tom C. Clark. Justices Felix Frankfurter and William J. Brennan concurred in a separate opinion.

Justice John M. Harlan wrote a dissenting opinion, in which Justices Stanley F. Reed and Harold H. Burton joined.

Jack Greenberg of New York and Peter A. Hall of Birmingham raised three questions in their appeal on behalf of Fikes. The first concerned the admission of the two confessions. Another dealt with the refusal of the trial judge to permit Fikes to testify about how the confessions were obtained and the third charged racial discrimination in the selection of the jury.

STATE HIGH COURT REVERSED

Chief Justice Warren said that, since the judgment of the Supreme Court of Alabama upholding the conviction must be reversed because of the admission of the confessions, it was unnecessary to decide the other two issues.

As the Chief Justice stated the facts in his opinion the daughter of the Mayor of Selma, Ala., was awakened in her apartment on the night of April 24, 1953, by an intruder. She found a Negro sitting on her with a knife at her throat. She struggled, seized the knife, and her assailant fled.

At the trial she did not identify Fikes as her assailant.

Fikes was arrested "on an open charge of investigation" on May 16, when police found him in an alley in a white neighborhood in Selma, Chief Justice Warren related. Fikes, he continued, was 27 years old at the time, had left school at 16 while in the third grade and was "a schizophrenic and highly suggestible." His mother testified that he had always been "thickheaded," it was added.

Describing the circumstances under which the confessions were obtained, the Chief Justice said:

"Here the prisoner was, an uneducated Negro, certainly of low mentality, if not mentally ill. ... for a period of a week he was kept in isolation, except for sessions of questioning. He saw no friend or relative. Both his father and a lawyer were barred from attempts to see him.

"The protections to be afforded to a prisoner upon preliminary hearing were denied him, contrary to the law of Alabama. He was questioned for several hours at a time over the course of five days preceding the first confession, and again interrogated at length before the written confession was secured.

"The totality of the circumstances that preceded the confessions in this case goes beyond the allowable limits. The use of the confessions secured in this setting was a denial of due process."

Justice Harlan, however, found nothing in the procedures that "violated due constitutional process."

"Concededly, there was no brutality or physical coercion," Judge Harlan stated, "And psychological coercion is by no means manifest."

Noting that the Supreme Court of Alabama had sustained the conviction, Justice Harlan declared that there was nothing in the record concerning the conduct of the state authorities that "does more than offend some fastidious squeamishness or private sentimentalism about combatting crime too energetically" and "due regard for the division between state and Federal functions requires that we let Alabama's judgment stand."

In another action today the Supreme Court granted a hearing to Jeremiah Reeves Jr., a Negro under death sentence for the rape of a white housewife in her home in Montgomery, Ala. Reeves charged that his trial was unfair because Negroes were systematically excluded from juries in Montgomery County and the public was kept out of the courtroom during the trial.

Author in Prison Wins Court Test

BY ALVIN SHUSTER | JUNE 11, 1957

Editor's Note: Despite many appeals, Caryl Chessman was executed in 1960.

WASHINGTON, JUNE 10 — The Supreme Court ordered a new lower court hearing today for a California criminal who has been under sentence to die in the gas chamber for nearly nine years.

In a 5-to-3 decision, the Court ruled that Caryl Chessman should have been represented at a Federal District Court hearing last year. The hearing was on the question of a new trial.

Chessman, who was convicted of attempted rape and kidnapping in 1948, had charged fraud in the preparation of the state court records of his original trial.

The Federal District Court ruled that there had been no fraud and turned down Chessman's appeal. Chessman then appealed anew to the Supreme Court.

DUE PROCESS HELD LACKING

Associate Justice John M. Harlan, speaking for the majority, said that because Chessman had not been represented he had been denied his constitutional right to due process of law.

"We think the petitioner [Chessman] was entitled to be represented throughout those proceedings either in person or by counsel," Mr. Harlan said.

He said that the majority had accepted the lower court's finding that there had been no fraud. But even so, he went on, Chessman never has had his day in court on the issue of validity of the record at his original trial.

"We must be deaf to all suggestions," he declared, "that a valid appeal to the Constitution, even by a guilty man, comes too late, because courts, including this court, were not earlier able to enforce what the Constitution demands.

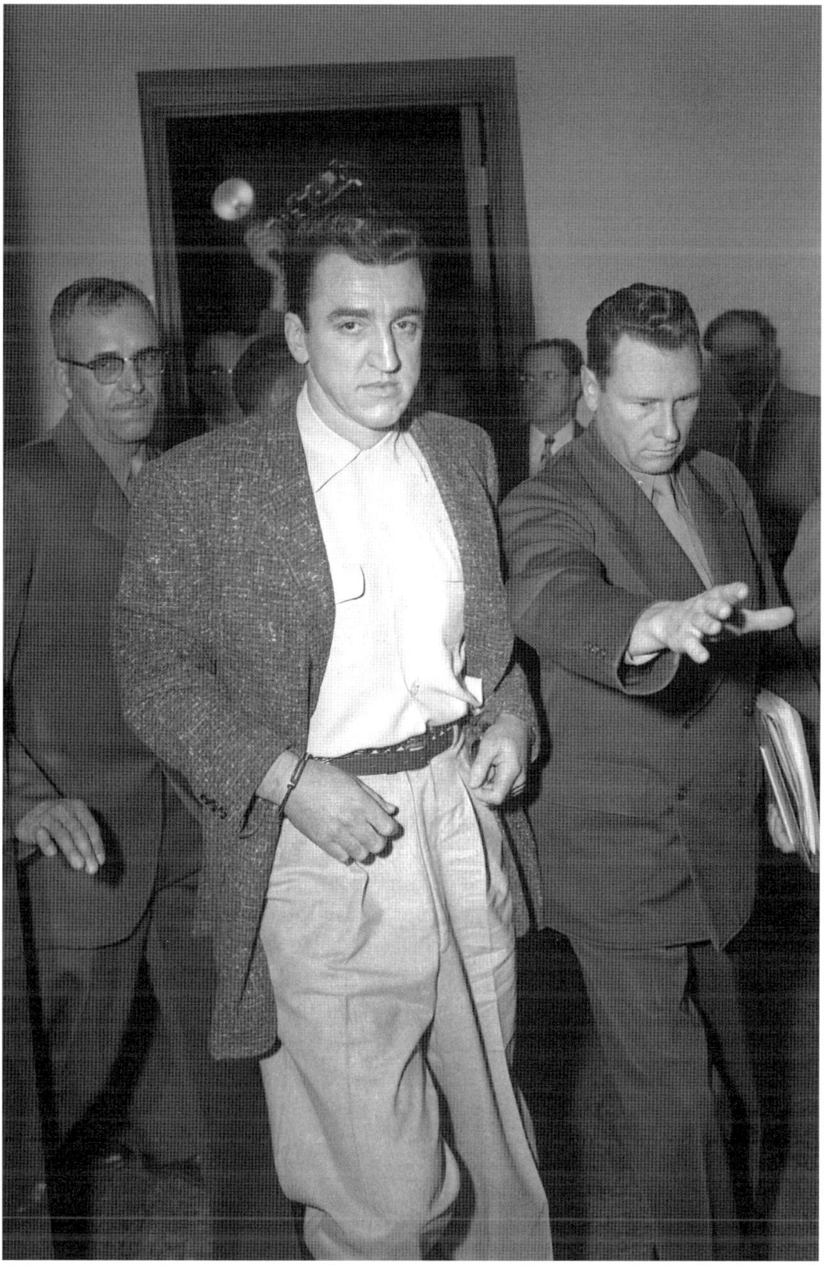

BETTMANN/GETTY IMAGES

Caryl Chessman, sentenced to death by the State of California. The Supreme Court ordered a new state court hearing on his case.

"The proponent before the court is not the petitioner, but the Constitution of the United States."

DOUGLAS SEES A STALL

In a strong dissent, Associate Justice William O. Douglas said Chessman "has received due process over and again." He declared that the "conclusion is irresistible that Chessman is playing a game with the courts, stalling for time while the facts of the case grow cold."

Associate Justice Tom Clark joined in Mr. Douglas' dissent. Associate Justice Harold H. Burton dissented in a separate one-paragraph comment in which he said Chessman had been accorded all his constitutional rights.

Joining Mr. Harlan in the majority were Associate Justices Hugo L. Black, Felix Frankfurter, William J. Brennan Jr. and Charles E. Whittaker. Chief Justice Earl Warren, a former Governor of California, took no part in the case.

TRANSCRIPT ATTACKED

Chessman's main argument is that the trial transcript that was submitted to the California Supreme Court on his appeal was "prejudicially incomplete and inadequate."

The issue arose after the original court reporter, Ernest R. Perry, died before he could transcribe all his shorthand notes. At the suggestion of the deputy district attorney, Stanley Fraser was hired to transcribe Mr. Perry's notes.

Justice Harlan noted that Mr Fraser, the substitute reporter, was an uncle by marriage of the deputy district attorney in charge of the case.

Chessman, who has acted as his own lawyer in several legal proceedings, was represented in the latest appeal by George T. Davis of San Francisco. William M. Bennett, deputy attorney general of California, submitted a brief on behalf of the state.

While in San Quentin Prison, Chessman wrote two books, "Cell 2455, Death Row," which became a best-seller, and "Trial by Ordeal," which did not.

Due Process

EDITORIAL | BY THE NEW YORK TIMES | AUG. 30, 1958

WHEN THE SUPREME COURT of the United States renders its decision in the Little Rock integration case, which was argued on Thursday, we may expect another important document in the history of American democracy. In the meantime we may rejoice that the Little Rock issue was dealt with, on this occasion, according to the principle of due process and not by bayonets. And when we say bayonets, let us not forget that bayonets were used in Little Rock to keep Negro boys and girls out of school before they were ever used, even symbolically, to protect the rights of those children to go to school.

While we wait for the court's decision, which is likely to be one of a long series in this field, we might give attention to the brief filed by the Justice Department on behalf of the United States — and presumably on behalf of all the children, as well as all the adults, of the United States. Among the principles that this excellent document set forth were the following: that the Government is concerned with the "maintenance of public education in accordance with the Constitution"; that violence does not justify a breach in constitutional rights; that good faith may be expected of all communities in carrying out the law of the land and the decisions of the courts; and that "the constitutional rights of some citizens may not be suspended or ignored because of the antagonistic acts of others."

President Eisenhower has been criticized for what seemed to be a justification of delay in the integration program in his news conference on Wednesday. He has, however, identified himself with this document of the Department of Justice to which we believe no reasonable man can honestly take exception.

The 'Due Process' Factor in the Meredith Case

OPINION | BY ARTHUR KROCK | OCT. 2, 1962

WASHINGTON, OCT. 1 — When the Supreme Court began its October term today it had already rejected, in effect and in fact, a pending appeal for review of the Meredith case by the state of Mississippi. In a most unusual, if not unparalleled, procedure, instead of dismissing the appeal as a judicial body in actual session, the members of the Supreme Court, from scattered locations during the summer recess, had given sanction to a single Justice, Hugo Black, to make the following statements in an order to the University of Mississippi to enroll James Meredith at the opening of the current semester:

> *... There is very little likelihood that this Court will grant certiorari to review the judgment of the Court of Appeals, which essentially involves only actual issues. ... Although convinced that I have the power to act alone in this matter, I have submitted it to each of my brethren, and I am authorized to state that each of them agrees that the case is properly before this Court, that I have power to act, and that, under the circumstances, I should exercise that power as I have done here.*

Established procedure under "due process" is completed only when a court of last resort has formally disposed of the final step available to litigants. Since the agreement of all the other Justices that Black announced in his order of Sept. 12, 1963, could have been learned only by communication means other than face-to-face discussion, this raises the legitimate question whether "due process" was afforded the state of Mississippi. If, as Justice Black also announced, the Court was certain to reject the state's request for review, that could have been done in the established manner when the Court reassembled today, the day Meredith actually was enrolled at the university.

BUYENLARGE/ARCHIVE PHOTOS/GETTY IMAGES

Federal marshals escorted James Meredith to his classes after Justice Black's order forced the University of Mississippi to accept Meredith's enrollment.

THE ATTORNEY GENERAL SPEAKS

On Sept. 29, in a speech telephoned to a San Francisco audience, Attorney General Kennedy chided the American Bar Association as well as the lawyers in Mississippi for the "absence of any expression of support ... for our [the Kennedy Administration's] present effort to deal with the situation. ..." It may be that the Supreme Court's highly unusual and informal manner of rejecting that state's final appeal will be attended by this same silence at the bar. But discussion of the method among lawyers would seem to be as obligatory on the profession as the support the Attorney General failed to receive from an official spokesman of the A.B.A.

His complaint was justified to that extent. Once the lower Federal court had imposed on the Mississippi state authorities obedience to its orders, as sustained — however irregularly — by Justice Black in the name of the Supreme Court, their execution by the Executive was mandatory if the constitutional system of the United States was to be maintained. And this absolute necessity is not lessened by the fact that the Constitution is what judges say it is, the Supreme Court has often rewritten and amended it, and also acted as a legislature, to effect shifting personal, social and economic doctrines.

THE DEPARTMENT'S ROLE

Both President Kennedy and his brother, the Attorney General, have no such claim for support for their politically based attempt to persuade the Democrats of the South that the Department of Justice's activities in the assault on racial segregation in the schools and colleges were purely responsive to Federal court orders after litigation instituted by private citizens. This attempt is plainly revealed in the stress the President and the Attorney General have given to the technical fact that "this Government had not originally been a party to" the Meredith case. But, after Federal Circuit Judge Cameron had granted four stays against the order of fellow-judges that Meredith must be enrolled in September, despite the pendency of Mississippi's appeal for review to the recessed Supreme Court, the Attorney General enthusiastically entered the proceedings before Black as *amicus curiae*.

As Anthony Lewis, this newspaper's chief reporter in this field, wrote in our issue of Sept. 2: "... The Justice Department has become increasingly active in school cases — especially since Mr. [Robert] Kennedy took office. From a starting point of intervening only when violence threatened compliance with a court order, the department has become more and more an initiator and planner of litigation."

ARTHUR KROCK is a reporter, Washington bureau chief and columnist for The New York Times.

Justice Black's Order

LETTER | THE NEW YORK TIMES | OCT. 12, 1962

Law professors deny the action raises issue of "due process."

TO THE EDITOR OF THE NEW YORK TIMES:

In his column "The 'Due Process' Factor in the Meredith Case," in the Oct. 2 Times, Arthur Krock asserted that the Supreme Court of the United States, acting through Justice Black, "rejected in effect and in fact a pending appeal for the review of the Meredith case by the state of Mississippi" and that the "most unusual, if not unparalleled, procedure" by which this was done "raises the legitimate question whether 'due process' was afforded the state of Mississippi." These implications of impropriety are misleading.

The judicial action which produced the "due process factor" in Mr. Krock's mind was a ruling issued by Justice Black on Sept. 10, 1962. This ruling resulted from a long sequence of events which began with Mr. Meredith's application for admission to the University of Mississippi in January, 1961, and culminated in a decision of the United States Court of Appeals on June 25, 1962, directing that Mr. Meredith be admitted. University officials sought a Supreme Court review of this decision by filing a petition for writ of certiorari which in normal course would not be acted upon until the Court convened for its new term in October.

COURT'S DISCRETION

Whether or not the Court will review a case on petition for writ of certiorari rests within its discretion, and comparatively few of such petitions are granted. It is common for a party who loses the decision in a lower court and petitions for writ of certiorari to ask the lower court to suspend or stay enforcement of the decision until it can be determined whether or not the case will be reviewed by the higher court.

The granting of such stays rests in the sound discretion of the court. In the Meredith case the Court of Appeals refused to grant such a stay.

That normally would have ended the matter unless the Supreme Court or one of its justices issued a stay. In the Meredith case, a Court of Appeals Judge, Judge Cameron, acting contrary to the views of his Brothers on the bench, purported to grant several such stays which the full court treated as ineffective and void.

In order to clear the record, particularly in view of the fact that Mr. Meredith wished to enter the university in September, his counsel filed the appropriate motion with Justice Black (the Supreme Court justice assigned to the Fifth Circuit for matters of this kind) asking that Judge Cameron's stay orders be vacated.

Justice Black's order granting this motion explicitly agreed with the reasons which led the Court of Appeals to deny a stay. He concluded his opinion as follows:

"Although convinced that I have the power to act alone in this matter, I have submitted it to each of my Brethren, and I am authorized to state that each of them agrees that the case is properly before this Court, that I have power to act, and that under the circumstances I should exercise that power as I have done here."

Justice Black's action was unusual only in the sense that fortunately the circumstances such as those he dealt with arise very infrequently; certainly there was nothing irregular in what he did.

CUSTOMARY PROCEDURE

Single justices have authority to act upon motions of this kind made when the Court is not in session, and indeed, this customary procedure for dealing with urgent matters is necessary for vacation-time, when the membership of the Court is scattered; in this case, there was special reason for speedy action since the fall term was about to begin at the university. His consultation with other members of the Court could not in any way prejudice the right of the university and appears to have been dictated by a desire to be certain that those rights were properly protected.

Furthermore, his action was not a final rejection of Mississippi's petition for review of the Meredith case; it only wiped from the record a stay order of a single lower court judge which that judge's own Brethren of the Court of Appeals did not regard as valid.

There is no justification whatever for the suggestion that Justice Black's conduct raises the slightest issue of "due process" in judicial procedure.

It is regrettable indeed that such an unfounded suggestion should be propagated by the pen of a columnist of the standing of Mr. Krock particularly at a time when such loose charges might be used to justify defiance of law.

PAUL W. BRUTON, **JOHN O. HONNOLD JR.**, **PAUL J. MISHKIN**,
The Law School, University of Pennsylvania,
Philadelphia, Oct. 4, 1962.

Close Decision in 'Lost Citizenship' Cases

OPINION | BY ARTHUR KROCK | FEB. 21, 1963

WASHINGTON, FEB. 20 — The effect of the 5 to 4 Supreme Court decision in the citizen "draft-dodger" cases this week was to deny to Congress the constitutional power to restrain draft-dodging by making loss of citizenship its automatic consequence.

There were two citizen defendants in these cases. One, Francisco Mendoza-Martinez, on his own admission went in 1942 to Mexico, where because of his parentage he also was a citizen, to evade military service in the United States, then at war. On his voluntary return in 1946 he was tried, convicted and served one year and a day for draft evasion. But five years later he was ordered deported on the ground that his stay in Mexico extended beyond Sept. 27, 1944, when Congress' automatic loss-of-citizenship penalty for draft evasion became effective. The other, Joseph Henry Cort, after registering for the draft, went to England for a university research job, and thereafter dictated to the United States the terms on which he would comply. When, in Cort's judgment, the national psychology finally had restored the prospect of a fair trial in this country, his application for a passport to permit his return was denied on the ground that his repeated noncompliance had automatically forfeited his citizenship under the terms of the existing Federal statutes.

'DUE-PROCESS' RESTRICTION

But, citizenship, said the one-man majority created by freshman Associate Justice Goldberg, cannot be terminated by these statutes: this can be done only after "due process of law." And "due process" in this context means formal indictment, trial and the rendering of a final affirmative verdict. Lacking this provision, said the majority, the existing statutes are "punitive," a legislative or executive gesture forbidden by the Constitution. “In legal contemplation, punitive, vindicative or exemplary damages are synonymous” (Bouvier’s Law Dictionary, Banks-Baldwin Publishing Co., 1948). And, since manifestly the purpose of the damages Congress prescribed for citizens who evaded their legally-imposed duty to their country in a crisis of security was in part “exemplary,” this provided the majority with the “incidental” ground on which it struck down the statutes.

This major factor of difference between the 5 and the 4 in evaluating the constitutional issue was best reflected in the following from Justice Stewart’s strong dissent:

> *The question of whether a statute is punitive ultimately depends upon whether the disability it imposes is for the purpose of vengeance or deterrence, of whether the disability is but an incident to some broader regulatory objective ... This legislation dealt with a problem of wartime morale reaching far beyond concern for any individual affected. (It) applies only to those who have left this country or remained outside of it for the purpose of avoiding the draft ... It is hardly an improvident exercise of constitutional power for Congress to disown those who have disowned this nation in time of ultimate need.*

FATAL INFECTION

There were less fundamental but nevertheless important disagreements among the justices. One was over a speculation whether a lower Federal court, which held that Cort had remained out of the United States to evade military service, was influenced to this judgment by the “presumption” expressed in the statutes that noncompliance plus absence from the country demonstrated evasion. The lower court did not mention this passage in its ruling. But it acquired importance in the opinions because Justice Stewart, though upholding the exercise of the existing statutes, concluded that this “presumption” had “fatally infected the administrative determination” that Cort had lost his citizenship. Of the other dissenters, however, Justice Harlan and Justice Clark saw “nothing constitutionally wrong with this (presumption) provision," and therefore with any effect it may have had.

Some Supreme Court crystal-gazers hold that, if Congress will rewrite the loss-of-citizenship statutes with a hypocritical preamble that they are not "punitively" conceived, the court will sustain them. Meanwhile, the citizen status of draft-dodgers, either in time of national emergency or war, may not on that account be terminated solely by Federal legislative or executive action.

ARTHUR KROCK is a reporter, Washington bureau chief and columnist for The New York Times.

Supreme Court Extends Ruling on Free Counsel

BY ANTHONY J. LEWIS | MARCH 19, 1963

WASHINGTON, MARCH 18 — The Supreme Court held today that the states must supply free lawyers to all poor persons facing serious criminal charges.

The court unanimously overruled its own 1942 decision in the landmark case of Betts v. Brady. There the ruling was that the Constitution required appointed counsel only in cases involving a death sentence or "special circumstances," such as an illiterate defendant.

Justice Hugo L. Black, who dissented in 1942, wrote the opinion for the majority today. He said Betts v. Brady was incorrectly decided.

"Reason and reflection," Justice Black said, "require us to recognize that in our adversary system of criminal justice any person haled into court who is too poor to hire a lawyer cannot be assured a fair trial unless counsel is provided for him. This seems to us to be an obvious truth."

FLORIDA CASE INVOLVED

The decision, one of the most important ever made by the Supreme Court in the criminal law field, was provoked by Clarence Earl Gideon, a 52-year-old inmate of the Florida State Prison.

Gideon was convicted of breaking and entering the Bay Harbor Poolroom in Panama City, Fla., with intent to commit petty larceny. He asked for a lawyer at his trial but was turned down.

The Florida Supreme Court rejected a habeas corpus petition from Gideon. He then sent a hand-written petition to the United States Supreme Court, which agreed to hear the case and to reconsider the correctness of Betts v. Brady.

At present only five states have no regular provision for appointment of counsel except in capital cases — those with possible death sentences. These states are, Florida, Alabama, Mississippi and North and South Carolina.

In a number of other states, however, appointing practices vary according to localities, with no regular provision in less populous areas for non-capital cases. And quite a few states do not provide counsel in misdemeanors or petty offenses.

MANY COULD ASK RELEASE

Thus today's decision could have a great impact across the country. Among other things it could permit many thousands of persons now in prison to demand new trials.

Justice Black's opinion did not say whether the new constitutional doctrine was to be applied to those already jailed. But there was nothing to indicate that others in Gideon's position could not seek their release on habeas corpus as he did, because he had no lawyer at his trial.

Florida estimated, in this case, that perhaps 5,000 prisoners in her jails had had no lawyers at their trials and might ask for release. The state made this a strong ground for pleading with the court not to overturn Betts v. Brady.

One restriction on the effect of the decision may be the doctrine of waiver — the rule that a man may waive his right to a lawyer by not demanding one. Gideon specifically asked for a lawyer at this trial, but many prisoners may not have done so.

Justice Black's decision did not settle, either, whether the new rule will apply to the most petty crimes, such as traffic offenses. That will presumably be worked out in later cases.

'RESPECTFUL BURIAL'

Justice John Marshall Harlan, in a concurring opinion, said he agreed that Betts v. Brady should be overruled but thought it deserved "a more respectful burial" than Justice Black's opinion saying it was wrong to start with.

Justice Harlan was persuaded by the fact that the Supreme Court in recent years had repeatedly found "special circumstances" requiring counsel. He said that "to continue a rule which is honored by this court only with lip service is not a healthy thing."

Justice Tom C. Clark also filed a separate concurrence, based on his conclusion that the Constitution made no distinction between capital and non-capital crimes.

In several other cases today the court took major steps to provide new protections for state criminal defendants.

It held, 6 to 3, that when a state provides a right to appeal criminal convictions, it must supply counsel on appeal for indigents. The dissenters were Justices Harlan, Clark and Potter Stewart.

The Justices divided 5 to 4 in deciding that Washington State had not given two prisoners an adequate record of their trial as a basis for appeal. Justice Byron White wrote the dissent, joined by Justices Harlan, Clark and Stewart.

A unanimous decision struck down an Indiana procedure under which the public defender might prevent a poor man from appealing by declaring the appeal frivolous.

By a vote of 6 to 3, with Justices Harlan, Clark and Stewart dissenting, the court held that Federal courts may release on habeas corpus a state prisoner who was turned down in the state courts because he failed to follow required procedure.

This case, which has great significance for the relations of state and Federal courts, involved Charles Noia of New York, serving a life sentence for murder.

Two co-defendants of Noia's were eventually released because confessions were found to have been coerced from all three. But Noia had never appealed — because, he said, he feared a death sentence in a new trial.

The New York courts said this failure to appeal barred any relief for him after his co-defendants went free. The Supreme Court said today that, whatever restricted the New York judiciary, Federal courts could and should free Noia.

Finally, by a vote of 5 to 4, the court said an Indiana prisoner should have a full hearing before a Federal court on his assertion that he had confessed after he was given a "truth serum" drug.

The dissenters — Justices Stewart, Harlan, Clark and White — agreed that a confession obtained by drugs would be invalid. But they said the prisoner had had ample chance to prove his claim in the state criminal proceedings, failed and should not be given a new chance in the Federal courts.

This barrage of criminal law decisions, especially the Gideon case, should spur state efforts to set up new methods of providing counsel for indigents.

Miranda v. Arizona

BY THE NEW YORK TIMES | OCT. 2, 1966

THE MIRANDA DECISION of the Supreme Court takes its name from one of four cases in which the Court last June 13 reversed convictions of men who had confessed to crimes of rape, robbery and murder. In the best-known case, Ernesto A. Miranda, a 25-year-old mentally retarded Arizonan, was convicted of kidnapping and raping an 18-year-old girl and received concurrent 20-to-30-year sentences. After having been identified in the police lineup by the girl, he had admitted the crime but he was not effectively warned of his right to counsel or that his statements could be used against him.

The principals in the three other cases were:

Michael Vignera, sentenced in Kings County Court, N.Y., to 30-to-60 years' imprisonment for robbing a Brooklyn dress shop. He had been detained 24 hours before the police brought him before a judge, and he had been held for about 12 hours before he had confessed. He was not advised of his right to counsel or other rights.

Carl Calvin Westover, sentenced in San Francisco to 15 years' imprisonment for the armed robbery of a bank and two savings and loan associations in Sacramento. He had been informed of his right to counsel but was held incommunicado and had no opportunity to obtain a lawyer during his 17 hours of interrogation.

Roy Allen Stewart, sentenced to death in Los Angeles after being convicted of robbery and murder in a purse-snatching in which the victim died of injuries. He had been held for five days during which, except for one confrontation by an accuser, he had seen no one but the police. He was questioned nine different times and confessed during the ninth interrogation; there was no indication that he had at any time been advised of his rights.

In the 5-to-4 decision reversing Miranda's conviction, Chief Justice Earl Warren delivered the majority opinion, declaring: "We hold that

BETTMANN/GETTY IMAGES

Ernesto Miranda, right, with his attorney John J. Flynn.

when an individual is taken into custody or otherwise deprived of his freedom by the authorities and is subjected to questioning, the privilege against self-incrimination is jeopardized. Procedural safeguards must be employed to protect the privilege ..."

Bitter dissents were filed by Justices Tom C. Clark, John M. Harlan, Potter Stewart and Byron R. White. In his opinion. Justice White observed: "More than the human dignity of the accused is involved; the human personality of others in the society must also be preserved. Thus the values reflected by the privilege are not the sole desideratum; society's interest in the general security is of equal weight."

CHAPTER 4

Perspectives Shift in the Late 20th Century

After Chief Justice Warren's retirement, rights such as the right to remain silent were strengthened in subsequent Supreme Court cases, but the meaning of due process continued to be debated in both criminal proceedings and other contexts. The extent of due process was examined in cases related to immigrants' rights, seizure of property and even a divorce case. Meanwhile, the constitutional basis for the right to privacy, and its relation to the due process clause, became a sticking point after the landmark Roe v. Wade decision (1973) and subsequent abortion cases.

Prosecutors Here Are Divided 3 to 2 on Jury Trials for Misdemeanors Subject to a Year's Sentence

BY ROBERT E. TOMASSON | JAN. 19, 1970

NEW YORK CITY'S POSITION as the only remaining legal jurisdiction in the nation that denies a jury trial to a defendant facing up to a year in jail has sharply divided the city's chief prosecutors.

In Nassau and Suffolk Counties, upstate New York and throughout the 49 other states, a defendant charged with a misdemeanor carrying up to a year's imprisonment upon conviction can demand — and receive as his right — a trial by jury.

But in the five boroughs of the country's largest city, the 86 Criminal Court judges are prevented from allowing a jury to decide a defendant's guilt of the so-called minor crimes.

The United States Supreme Court now has under consideration a case that will decide whether New York City is to retain its anomalous role in criminal law or be made to conform with the rest of the nation.

COURT CROWDING A FACTOR

Attorney General Louis J. Lefkowitz has led the opposition to granting jury trials in misdemeanor cases with the warning that if they are allowed the already crowded Criminal Courts could become all but inoperable under present facilities.

District Attorney Frank S. Hogan of Manhattan and District Attorney Burton B. Roberts of the Bronx strongly support this view. But the city's three other District Attorneys — Thomas J. Mackell of Queens, Eugene Gold of Brooklyn and John M. Braisted Jr. of Staten Island — are in favor of letting a jury decide if a man is to be jailed for as long as a year.

An argument that has been used to counter the apprehension of officials over extending the right to a jury trial has been the experience of California, which allows jury trials if a person can be penalized at all — even for jaywalking — regardless of whether he can be sent to jail for any length of time.

In Los Angeles County, which has an arrest figure roughly comparable to New York City's — around 150,000 a year — most individuals either plead guilty or waive jury trials in the less serious cases.

The case that will decide the issue is Baldwin v. New York, which was argued Dec. 9 before the nine justices of the Supreme Court. It involves the unsuccessful attempt of a 24-year-old defendant to obtain a jury trial in a pickpocket incident.

1968 DECISION RECALLED

The decision, it is expected, will clarify a landmark decision handed down by the court May 20, 1968, that all states must grant jury trials in cases involving possible jail sentences of up to two years. The court added that a jury did not have to sit in a case where the maximum possible sentence was six months.

In a footnote to that case, Duncan v. Louisiana, Justice Byron R. White noted that "there appear to be only two instances, aside from the Louisiana scheme, in which state denies a jury trial for crime punishable by imprisonment for longer than six months." The other jurisdictions were New Jersey and New York City.

The Duncan decision deliberately refrained, Justice White wrote, from setting "the exact location of the line between" the permissible nonjury provision in six-month cases and the mandatory requirement for juries for crimes involving possible two-year sentences.

In June, 1968, the New Jersey Legislature, rather than face the possibility of being compelled to grant jury trials in one-year-sentence cases, adopted the simple expedient of reducing to six months the one crime — disorderly conduct — that was punishable by maximum sentence of a year without a jury trial.

CLASS A MISDEMEANORS

In New York City, however, there are scores of so-called class "A" misdemeanors which carry a year's sentence. They include several types of minor physical assault, thefts of various types and a wide range of property damage.

The circumstances of the two cases seem to belie the profound constitutional issue involved in an accused man's right to a jury trial.

The Duncan case began in Plaquemines Parish, Louisiana, in October, 1966, while the Baldwin case had its origins on a crowded escalator in the Port Authority Bus Terminal in midtown Manhattan in August, 1968.

Justice White gave this account of the Duncan case:

Gary Duncan, 19 years old, was driving on Highway 23 when he spotted two cousins "engaged in a conversation by the side of the road with four white boys."

Knowing that his cousins, who had recently transferred to a formerly all-white high school, had reported the occurrence of racial incidents at the school, Duncan stopped the car, got out, and approached the six boys.

The trial testimony in the local court, Justice White noted, "was in dispute on many points," with "the whites" testifying that Duncan "slapped Herman Landry, one of the white boys on the elbow."

DUNCAN GOT 60 DAYS

The local trial judge found young Duncan guilty of simple battery and sentenced him to 60 days in jail.

One edict the High Court set in reversing the conviction was that the governing factor was not the amount of time the defendant was sentenced to serve, but the amount of time he could have received. While Gary Duncan received only 60 days, the law he was accused of violating carried a maximum two-year sentence.

On a hot August evening almost two years later, Robert Baldwin and a friend entered the bustling Port Authority terminal where they proceeded to one of the escalators.

A shout from a woman brought a policeman, who arrested Baldwin and charged him with jostling, a term used to describe, among other things, a pickpocket caught in the act.

He was convicted under the misdemeanor statute after he was denied a jury trial, and sentenced to a year in jail.

In reversing the Duncan conviction, Justice White wrote for the majority that the 14th Amendment to the Constitution guarantees the right of a jury trial in all criminal cases which, if they were tried in a Federal court, would come within the Sixth Amendment's guaranty of a jury trial.

In evoking the system used in the Federal system, Justice White said that the determining factor in allowing state jury trials is whether the alleged crime is "petty" or "serious."

In the Federal courts, a petty crime is defined as one that carries a maximum sentence of six months for which no jury need sit.

LEGAL AID MAN'S VIEW

In the Baldwin case, William H. Hellerstein, the attorney-in-charge of the criminal appeals bureau of the Legal Aid Society, argued that the Duncan decision should apply to any cases involving a sentence of more than six months.

Michael R. Juviler, the assistant District Attorney in charge of the Manhattan appeals bureau, countered that one-year sentences do not constitute serious crimes and they should be decided by judges alone.

The Legal Aid official told the Supreme Court that the city's denial of jury trials stemmed in part from New York's original conservative colonial government.

Justice John M. Harlan, who is opposed to jury trials in misdemeanor cases, noted in the Duncan case that Alexander Hamilton, who signed the Constitution on behalf of New York, was strongly opposed to inclusion of the Bill of Rights, of which the states' jury trials are an important part.

In his argument, Mr. Juviler noted that nine states use the one-year penalty as a cutoff between having a 12-man or smaller jury and that the one-year period is recognized by other states as marking the distinction between serious and petty crimes.

For Gary Duncan, whose 60-day sentence was reversed, the constitutional issues may seem remote, for he has served his term. And for Robert Baldwin, whose one-year sentence is being reviewed, a legal victory may also seem hollow for he has served more than 10 months of his sentence and been released.

The Same Justice Can Be Both a 'Strict' and a 'Loose' Constructionist

BY ANTHONY LEWIS | MAY 24, 1970

THE YEAR IS 1972, and the Supreme Court has before it the first case testing the Preventive Detention Act of 1971. Passed by Congress at the urging of President Nixon, the act allows Federal judges to order persons accused of serious crimes to be held in prison until trial if their record indicates that they might commit further crimes while on bail. Hubert Johnson, a District of Columbia Negro charged with armed robbery, is being held under the act because he has several other felony convictions on his record. He wants the Supreme Court to declare his detention without bail unconstitutional.

Johnson's lawyer relies on the Eighth Amendment: "Excessive bail shall not be required ..." That language, he points out, has always been interpreted to mean that men accused of non-capital crimes must be given bail unless they seem likely to flee the jurisdiction. Successive courts, reading British and colonial history, have found that only the risk of flight — not the possibility of further criminal behavior — can justify the imposition of high bail or the withholding of bail altogether. In light of that conclusive history and consistent interpretation, the lawyer argues, the Supreme Court must apply the amendment strictly and strike down the new act.

Attorney General Mitchell argues that the Supreme Court cannot be bound by such a literal, historical reading of the Constitution: it must consider sociological changes. We are now a society of populous and unruly cities, not a Jeffersonian rural paradise, and language used in the 18th century must be reinterpreted in light of the new conditions. It is the very function of the Court to give the Constitution flexibility. It should weigh the exigencies of public safety that led Congress to enact the detention statute, take a less rigid view of the Eighth Amendment and uphold the act.

Fantasy? Not really. The Supreme Court could well be hearing arguments along those lines, if a preventive detention bill is passed by Congress. And who then would be the "strict constructionist"?

President Nixon has used the phrase in a political context, giving the impression that there are right and left ways of construing the Constitution. One method is strict, sound, conservative; the other loose, uncontrolled, liberal. His political response to the defeat of his two ill-chosen nominees to the Supreme Court, Clement Haynsworth and G. Harrold Carswell, was to blame for the defeat of liberals who, he said, are opposed in principle to "strict construction" of the Constitution.

The implication is that liberals import personal views into the Constitution when they interpret it, while conservatives go strictly by the original text. As newsman Tom Wicker put it, the President indicates that "a 'strict constructionist' is one who will abide by the Constitution, while others — say, those of the type that formed the Warren Court majority — are willing to distort it for their own social and political ends."

BUT THE EXAMPLE of preventive detention and the Eighth Amendment shows that things are not so simple. The labels liberal and conservative do not determine how a man approaches the job of interpreting the Constitution.

Taking the history of the Supreme Court as a whole, the more fanciful or extravagant interpreting has mostly been done on behalf of property rights — i.e., on the conservative side. Indeed, there is a whole line of decisions, over decades ending in 1937, that now seem to us to lack any reasonable basis in the text of the Constitution at all. They were pure web-spinning by judges determined to protect property.

The symbolic beginning was the case of Lochner v. New York, in 1905. New York had adopted a law limiting the work of bakers to 60 hours a week. The Supreme Court, by a vote of 5 to 4, found the law in violation of the 14th Amendment's provision that no state may "deprive any person of life, liberty or property without due process of law." The liberty involved, as the majority saw it, was something called "liberty of contract" — the right to buy or sell human labor. And so, to limit the hours worked in a trade that admittedly was dangerous to health denied the workers and employers their liberty.

"Statutes of the nature of that under review," said Mr. Justice Peckham, "limiting the hours in which grown and intelligent men may labor to earn their living, are mere meddlesome interferences with the rights of the individual."

Oliver Wendell Holmes Jr. had taken his seat on the Court a few years before. In economic theory he rather agreed with the majority's premise; he personally thought all efforts by governments to soften the rigors of the free market were doomed to fail. But as a judge he would not read his economic assumptions into the general language of the Constitution.

"The 14th Amendment does not enact Mr. Herbert Spencer's 'Social Statics'," he wrote in Lochner, bowing to the great free-market philosopher of the day. "A constitution is not intended to embody a particular economic theory, whether of paternalism and the organic relation of the citizen to the state or of laissez faire. It is made for people of fundamentally differing views, and the accident of our finding certain opinions natural and familiar, or novel and even shocking, ought not to conclude our judgment upon the question whether statutes embodying them conflict with the Constitution of the United States."

HOLMES RUNS THROUGH 30 years of property-worship on the Supreme Court as a voice of sanity amid madness. He was hailed as a liberal judge because he dissented against a majority that tried to read reactionary values into the text of the Constitution. But, of course, he would have said he was just a judge, doing as honest a job as he could.

The judges intent on protecting property and a laissez-faire economy tried to limit the Federal Government's power as well as the states'. The outstanding case concerned a Federal law against the shipment of goods made by child labor across state lines. Attempts by individual states to ban child labor had not worked well because of a variant on Gresham's Law: in states where children could still be worked all day in mines and mills, companies paid lower wages and undercut competitors. And so Congress invoked its power over interstate commerce to make a uniform national rule.

The Constitution in explicit language gives Congress authority to regulate interstate commerce. The Supreme Court, all the way back to John Marshall, had said this authority was complete, to be used as Congress decided. But in the child labor case in 1918, a 5-4 majority decided that Congress could not prohibit commerce in anything unless the thing itself was "evil." Holmes, noting that the Court had only recently upheld restrictions on commerce in alcoholic beverages, wrote:

"It is not for this Court to pronounce when prohibition is necessary … — to say that it is permissible as against strong drink, but not as against the product of ruined lives."

The due-process clause of the 14th Amendment was construed to prevent state safety and economic regulations by the score. In 1925, for example, a Pennsylvania law against the use of shoddy (shredded rags) in bedding was declared unconstitutional, and in 1928 a New York law limiting the profit of ticket agents was also struck down.

In 1930, when he was 89, Holmes wrote in dissent from a decision restricting the rights of the states to tax bondholders: "As the decisions now stand, I see hardly any limit but the sky to the invalidating of those [state] rights if they happen to strike a majority of this Court as for any reason undesirable. I cannot believe that the Amendment was intended to give us carte blanche to embody our economic or moral beliefs in its prohibitions."

NOW THERE ARE two interesting things about those cases in which Holmes developed the reputation of the great dissenter. One is that the majority views have sunk without trace. All those decisions have been overruled, and no serious person now thinks the general words of the Constitution place such tight restrictions on the power of the states to police business or of Congress to regulate commerce. Not even Richard Nixon could find a judge who believes that a state denies someone's constitutional "liberty" by barring the use of shoddy in bedding.

The other thing is that Holmes was not consistent. He wrote with unequaled eloquence, in these economic cases, of how wrong it was for a judge to construe the Constitution in the light of his personal beliefs. But when it came to freedom of speech, Holmes was prepared to do just what he had foresworn in economics — breathe into the Constitution what he thought was the essential philosophy of America.

The great example was the Abrams case, decided in 1919. Five rather pathetic socialists had been convicted under the Espionage Act, during World War I, for publishing two leaflets against the war. A majority sustained the convictions against a claim of protection under the First Amendment's guarantee of free speech. Holmes, joined by Brandeis, dissented.

"Persecution for the expression of opinions," he wrote, "seems to me perfectly logical. If you have no doubt of your premises or your power and want a certain result with all your heart, you naturally express your wishes in law and sweep away all opposition. …

"But when men have realized that time has upset many fighting faiths, they may come to believe even more than they believe the very foundations of their own conduct that the ultimate good desired is better reached by free trade in ideas — that the best test of truth is the power of the thought to get itself accepted in the competition of the market, and that truth is the only ground upon which their wishes safely can be carried out. That at any rate is the theory of our Constitution. It is an experiment, as all life is an experiment. …

"I think that we should be eternally vigilant against attempts to check the expression of opinions that we loathe and believe to be fraught with death. …"

That opinion has been quoted at some length because it is so striking in the freedom of its philosophizing — so broad, one can say, in its construction of what the Constitution prohibits. For Holmes, then, the Constitution guarantees free trade in ideas but not in economics. Why?

FELIX FRANKFURTER, worshiper of Holmes but at the same time a great exponent of consistent constitutional interpretation, struggled with the riddle. In 1949, as a member of the Court himself, he attempted an explanation:

"Those liberties of the individual which history has attested as the indispensable conditions of an open as against a closed society come to this Court with a momentum for respect lacking when appeal is made to liberties which derive merely from shifting economic arrangements. Accordingly, Mr. Justice Holmes was far more ready to find legislative invasion where free inquiry was involved than in the debatable area of economics."

But again, *whose* history has attested the Frankfurter conclusion? Would Marx agree that free speech is more important to a society than "shifting economic arrangements"? Is that any more than Felix Frankfurter's personal reading of Oliver Wendell Holmes's philosophical construction of the Constitution?

As a judge, Frankfurter was acutely self-conscious in interpreting the Constitution: not fearful of the duty, not at all, but recognizing the power inherent in the function. He became the apostle of "restraint" on the part of judges, the notion that courts should defer to elected politicians and find their laws constitutional if at all possible. He has even been praised by President Nixon — a considerable irony when one recalls the qualities of intellect and breadth of understanding that he wanted in Supreme Court justices, and imagines what he would have thought of Harrold Carswell.

But for all his talk of restraint, Justice Frankfurter was not really consistent in what he did as an expounder of the Constitution. When an issue came along that moved him, he could be as unrestrained as the next fellow.

Wiretapping was one of those issues: he tried for years to have the Court overrule a 1928 decision and bring tapping within the Fourth Amendment's strictures on police searches and seizures. (The Court did so after his death.) Searches were generally a sensitive subject for Frankfurter. In 1952 he wrote the opinion for a majority throwing out a narcotics conviction based on evidence forcibly pumped by the police from the suspect's stomach. Unable to pin his objections to a more specific phrase in the Constitution, Frankfurter held that the stomach pumping violated due process under the 14th Amendment because it was "conduct that shocks the conscience."

Frankfurter, applying his attitude of restraint, was ready to permit incursions on free speech that Holmes and Brandeis would surely have rejected — notably the prosecutions of Communists under the Smith Act. But when academic freedom was threatened, Frankfurter bridled; he would not let New Hampshire jail a lecturer for contempt for refusing to answer questions about the Progressive party of 1948. And freedom of religion was vital to him: he would have struck down many mixtures of church and state approved by a majority of his colleagues, such as released time for religious education and state aid to parochial school buses. He was even ready, most radically, to question the constitutionality of tax exemptions for church property.

The way Justice Frankfurter reached seemingly incongruous results in similar cases — on free speech, for example — was by weighing the conflicting interests involved as he saw them.

Thus in 1951, when the Court first upheld convictions of Communist leaders for conspiring to advocate overthrow of the Government by force, Justice Frankfurter said: "On any scale of values which we have hitherto recognized, speech of this sort ranks low." He said the Communist party was a serious enough organization so that Congress could rationally regard it as a threat to security; and Congress, he concluded, must be allowed to do much that might seem "illiberal because repressive and envenoming." But when he came in 1957 to the case of the New Hampshire lecturer, Justice Frankfurter evidently found the value of the speech at issue greater, and New Hampshire's security interest less.

Even the philosopher of judicial deference, then, does not by his record give us a clear definition of "strict construction." Nor is our confusion eased when we consider the powerful views of the other great figure on the modern Supreme Court, Hugo L. Black.

MR. BLACK IS by his own terms the most uncompromising "strict constructionist" in the history of the Court. More than any other judge in memory, he claims to base his decisions on the literal text of the Constitution. As he put it just a few weeks ago:

"I believe the Court has no power to add to or subtract from the procedures set forth by the Founders [in the Constitution] ... I shall not at any time surrender my belief that that document itself should be our guide, not our own concept of what is fair, decent and right."

Justice Hugo LaFayette Black.

The issue in the case that Justice Black was commenting upon will indicate how far he is prepared to carry his view. It was whether a juvenile court, trying a child for what would be a criminal offense for an adult, must find proof of the offense beyond a reasonable doubt. A majority said yes; two dissenters said no. Justice Black alone argued that there was no requirement of proof beyond a reasonable doubt in any criminal trial, adult or juvenile. Even though that standard had universally applied in American history, he said, and even though many Supreme Court opinions had treated it as an essential part of "due process," it was not specifically mentioned in the Constitution along with jury trial and the right to counsel and so was not to be protected.

There are passages of Hugo Black's that could be used by Spiro Agnew, if he did not worry about the context. In that stomach-pumping case, Black derided the majority concept that an act that "shocks the conscience" denies due process. "What avenues of investigation," he asked, "are open to discover canons of conduct so universally favored that this Court should write them into the Constitution?" His colleagues, he charged, were really just reading their own prejudices into the due process clause. He rejected "the accordion like qualities of this philosophy."

But the irony is that Justice Black has been the greatest innovating judge of the century, responsible more than any other man for the new role of the Supreme Court as a force for social change. Can he be what President Nixon has in mind when he talks of a "strict constructionist"?

BLACK INSISTS THAT everything he has done, by way of constitutional doctrine, has come from a strict reading of the text. The familiar example is speech. The First Amendment, Black emphasizes, says: "Congress shall make no law … abridging the freedom of speech"; that means absolutely "no law." On that premise Black has based his implacable opposition to loyalty oaths, prosecution of Communists and suppression of obscenity — positions that once seemed radical but have now all been adopted by the Supreme Court except possibly for a small remaining resistance to hard-core pornography.

Similarly, in the field of criminal law, Justice Black has led the movement toward greater Federal judicial control of local police practices — the movement that President Nixon made a campaign target in 1968. Black has done so by reaching the historical conclusion that the due-process clause of the 14th Amendment was intended to apply verbatim to the states all of the first eight amendments in the Bill of Rights, which originally restricted only Congress. Thus, he insisted that state criminal defendants have an absolute right to counsel, the right not to testify against themselves, and so on. In the last decade the Supreme Court has adopted these conclusions, though on less rigid reasoning than Black's.

But Justice Black's most significant single contribution to constitutional law — or so it seems to me — was not based on a literal or historical reading of the text. That is the one-man one-vote doctrine that has brought a revolutionary redistricting of every American state legislature. It began with a Black dissent in 1946. In 1964 Chief Justice Warren, for a majority, adopted the rule that the districts in every state legislative house must be essentially equal in population. The decision was based on the 14th Amendment's clause assuring every person "the equal protection of the laws," and no one contradicted Justice Harlan's statement in dissent that there was no historical association of that clause with the gerrymandering problem. The decision was simply judicial statesmanship of a high order, applying old words to a new problem in light of generally accepted American ideals. That is the very method of judging-in-the-large that Black disclaims, but here he did not say nay.

In any case, it is easy enough to show that Justice Black has not really applied in a mechanical way the absolutes he claims to find in the Constitution. Some demonstrations are "speech" for him, but others move outside that label and become subject to official control and repression. The First Amendment's ban on any establishment of religion did not prevent New Jersey from financing parochial school buses, in Black's reading; his disposition of the problem is almost a parody of mechanical constitutional interpretation:

"The First Amendment has erected a wall between church and state. That wall must be kept high and impregnable. We could not approve the slightest breach. New Jersey has not breached it here."

AND SO WE SEE that neither Justice Black nor Justice Frankfurter found a magic key to strict construction of the Constitution. But that should surprise no one who thinks about the problem just a little. For the brief text left us by those noble-minded 18th century draftsmen, and the subsequent amendments, do not lend themselves to automatic readings.

What is a strict construction of "commerce among the several states," or "due process of law," or "equal protection of the laws"? Those phrases, as Judge Learned Hand said, are empty vessels. They can be given meaning only by being applied to concrete facts in specific cases. That is the function of the justices.

Rigidity in a written constitution would have been fatal to the enterprise. The American Constitution has survived, while so many others have failed, because it was written in open language and interpreted in a flexible way by successive generations of judges. It was a constitution, Chief Justice Marshall said, "intended to endure for ages to come, and consequently to be adapted to the various crises of human affairs."

The mention of Marshall is a reminder that the argument about "strict construction" is subject to one major confusion. Today, as in the cases concerned with the rights of criminal suspects, the emphasis of the Court's work is on protecting individuals against the weight of power from all government. In Marshall's day the great issue was the allocation of power between the Federal Government on the one hand and the states on the other. And the difference is fundamental.

Marshall gave an expansive reading to those clauses in which the Framers, fearful of Federal authority, had carefully listed the limited powers of the new national Government. The strict constructionists of his day were states'-rights men. If they had prevailed, the result would have been to deny power to the Federal Government. Today, in the Nixon political view of what "strict construction" means, it would enhance the power of the Federal and state governments over criminal defendants, demonstrators, blacks and the like.

Over history, in fact, the Supreme Court has played a dual role: it has enlarged the powers of government to deal with increasingly complicated social problems; it has also enlarged the citizen's protections against official abuse.

In that course, the Court has seldom had a majority of what by any definition could be called "strict constructionists." Its judges have mostly felt they had a duty to apply their own best understanding of America's fundamental beliefs to flesh out the language of the Constitution in deciding contemporary problems. That was probably inevitable: it was in the nature of the text and of the judges' unparalleled power to strike down the acts of elected legislatures and officials.

What has mattered, in the end, is whether the judges read the country's spirit right. Majorities on the Supreme Court thought it was fundamentally wrong — unconstitutional — to have paper money, or an income tax, or minimum wages. The country disagreed, and those decisions turned to dust. "Their power is enormous," Tocqueville said of the justices, "but it is the power of public opinion."

Understanding, then, is what our system requires of Supreme Court justices — not adherence to a formula. Understanding, and intellectual honesty in analyzing difficult problems, and imagination, and modesty derived from historical perspective, and, not least, the ability to articulate persuasive reasons for a judgment.

THERE WAS A fair statement of the problem a few years ago by Mr. Justice White, dissenting in the famous Miranda case. The majority held that, before the police may question a criminal suspect who is in custody, they must tell him that he has a right to remain silent, that anything he says may be used against him and that he has an immediate right to a lawyer — free, if he is poor. Byron White said:

"That the Court's holding today is neither compelled nor even strongly suggested by the language of the Fifth Amendment [the self-incrimination clause], is at odds with American and English legal history, and involves a departure from a long line of precedent does not prove either that the Court has exceeded its powers or that the Court is wrong or unwise ...

"What it has done is to make new law and new public policy in much the same way that it has in the course of interpreting other great clauses of the Constitution. This is what the Court historically has done. Indeed, it is what it must do and will continue to do until and unless there is some fundamental change in the constitutional distribution of governmental powers ...

"But it is wholly legitimate to examine the mode of this or any other constitutional decision in this Court and to inquire into the advisability of its end-product in terms of the long-range interest of the country. At the very least the Court's text and reasoning should withstand analysis and be a fair exposition of the constitutional provision which its opinion interprets. Decisions like these cannot rest alone on syllogism, metaphysics or some ill-defined notions of natural justice, although each will perhaps play its part ..."

It is in those terms that a constitutional decision must be judged, not in simple epithets like "strict construction" — nor, one must add, in gushings over a sympathetic human result without regard to the judge's reasoning.

To take the Miranda case as an example, I found myself among the critics because Chief Justice Warren's opinion did not seem to me to meet Justice White's tests for a groundbreaking decision. It did not demonstrate compelling reasons in logic or experience for a significant change in the standards of criminal justice. It did not show any moral or political vacuum in the community that made judicial action urgent, as in the legislative-districting cases. And it did not lay out thoroughly or fairly the practical considerations that had to be canvassed; as one instance, the opinion suggested that English practice assured suspects of counsel before being questioned, whereas the opposite is in fact true.

But it must be admitted that not even the most objective and complete analysis would necessarily change the result. Judges, like the rest of us, are moved by inarticulate premises — attitudes that determine their whole approach to an issue like that presented in Miranda. One judge may be acutely sensitive, because of his life's experience, to the dangers of crime, another to the risk of unfairness toward poor suspects. If all President Nixon really means is that he wants judges especially concerned about crime, it is of course his right to apply that standard. But there is no mechanical formula that can govern a judge's attitude toward constitutional decision generally.

To make the law for a continental nation is an unimaginable responsibility for any man, not least a judge appointed for life. To recognize what is involved, as Justice White did with such unusual candor, is the beginning of humility and wisdom.

President Nixon's third choice for this seat on the Supreme Court, Harry A. Blackmun, quite clearly understands the weight he has been chosen to bear. For on the United States Court of Appeals he has said, in important cases, that it was not his function as an inferior judge to make new constitutional law; that was the function of the Supreme Court.

Justice Blackmun has got off to a good start in his new responsibility in at least one respect. When asked whether he was a "strict constructionist," he answered: "Oh, that's a label. I don't know what it means."

ANTHONY LEWIS, chief of this newspaper's London bureau, formerly covered the Supreme Court for The Times.

High Court Upsets a State's Trial Rules

BY WARREN WEAVER JR. | FEB. 25, 1973

WASHINGTON, FEB. 24 — In a decision that could have a broad national impact on the criminal justice system, the Supreme Court has ordered a new trial for a Mississippi black convicted of murdering a policeman.

The 8-to-1 ruling this week clearly suggested that the Court would not hesitate to invalidate state rules of evidence in criminal cases where the Justices find that such rules have interfered with the constitutional right of the accused to a fair trial.

Associate Justice Lewis F. Powell Jr., the author of the majority opinion, made a special effort to emphasize that he did not intend to introduce any sweeping changes into criminal law procedure, but some lawyers interpreted the decision as having considerably wider scope.

"In reaching this judgment," Justice Powell wrote, "we establish no new principles of constitutional law. Nor does our holding signal any diminution in the respect traditionally accorded to the states in the establishment and implementation of their own criminal trial rules and procedures."

"Rather, we hold quite simply that under the facts and circumstances of this case the rulings of the trial court deprived Chambers of a fair trial," he concluded.

The defendant in the case, Leon Chambers, was found guilty of the slaying in 1969 of Aaron Liberty, a Woodville, Miss., policeman, despite the fact that another man, Gable McDonald, had confessed to the crime four times, once in a signed statement later repudiated and three times in private conversation.

But, under Mississippi procedure, Chambers's attorney could not introduce evidence of the three oral confessions since they would constitute hearsay and was unable to cross-examine McDonald because he was not called as a prosecution witness.

In a carefully reasoned 18-page opinion, the Supreme Court majority struck down both these limitations on an accused criminal's ability to defend himself, certainly in similar future cases in Mississippi and by implication where such limits exist elsewhere.

RIGHT TO CROSS-EXAMINE

"The availability of the right to confront and to cross-examine those who give damaging testimony against the accused has never been held to depend on whether the witness was initially put on the stand by the accused or by the state," Justice Powell wrote.

"We reject the notion that a right of such substance in the criminal process may be governed by that technicality or by any narrow and unrealistic definition of the word 'against.' "

As to barring the testimony of the three men to whom McDonald confessed, the high court said that their evidence "was critical to Chambers's defense."

"In these circumstances, where constitutional rights directly affecting the ascertainment of guilt are implicated, the hearsay rule may not be applied mechanistically to defeat the ends of justice," the Court concluded.

Peter Westen, a Washington lawyer who handled the Chambers appeal for the Lawyers Committee on Civil Rights, said he believed that Justice Powell's decision, despite its self-limiting language, had established two new principles of constitutional law:

• That an accused can cross-examine any witness, including his own, when their testimony tends to prejudice his defense, despite contrary state laws.

• That a criminal defendant has a constitutional right to offer evidence of his innocence, even when it is inadmissible under state bans against hearsay and possibly when it runs counter to other types of state restriction.

There was some irony in the fact that three of President Nixon's four appointees to the Court — Chief Justice Warren E. Burger and Associate Justices Harry A. Blackmun and Powell — all supported a decision that seems likely to make the prosecutor's job somewhat harder and the defendant's easier.

Mr. Nixon has twice campaigned as a supporter of tougher law enforcement and as a critic of Federal judges who raise overly nice constitutional obstacles to state attempts at controlling crime.

The sole dissenter, Associate Justice William H. Rehnquist, argued that Chambers was not entitled to a new trial because he did not make any constitutional objections at his original trial and thus could not raise them for the first time on appeal.

High Court Strengthens Right to Silence at Arrest

SPECIAL TO THE NEW YORK TIMES | JUNE 18, 1976

WASHINGTON, JUNE 18 — The Supreme Court held today that a defendant's silence after being advised of his right to remain silent under questioning could not be used against him in a trial.

Ruling 6 to 3 in favor of two men convicted in Ohio marijuana cases, the Court based its decision on the landmark 1966 Miranda ruling requiring that suspects be informed of their rights before being questioned.

Specifically, the Court ruled that if a defendant is warned at his arrest of his right to remain silent, as required by the Miranda decision, and if he then does not give his exculpatory story until the trial, the prosecutor may not try to shake the story by cross-examining the defendant about why he did not tell the story when he was first arrested.

To allow the prosecutor to do this, the Court said in an opinion by Associate Justice Lewis F. Powell Jr., would be "fundamentally unfair" and would violate the defendant's right to due process.

The Court has itself been criticized for some rulings that appear to have eroded the Miranda decision various ways. But it based its ruling today on its 1966 ruling, saying, in part, that the so-called "Miranda warnings" carry an "implicit" assurance that silence will carry no penalty.

It also noted that a defendant's silence after his arrest may "be nothing more than the arrestee's exercise of these Miranda rights," rather than proof of anything.

In a second case today, the Court ruled, 6 to 2, that a guilty plea must be set aside, as a violation of the due process guarantee, if the defendant had not been given adequate notice of a critical element of the offense to which he was pleading.

NEW YORK CASE

The decision, written by Associate Justice John Paul Stevens, came in a New York case in which the defendant had pleaded guilty to second-degree murder but had not been advised that one of the elements of that offense — and thus an element that he was admitting — was intent to kill.

However, the high court rejected allegations of due process violations in a third case, involving Wisconsin school teachers who were dismissed by the local school board after they went on strike when collective bargaining negotiations between the teachers and the school board broke down.

The Court held that teachers had no due process right to have someone else, more impartial than the school board, decide whether they should be dismissed for striking.

The decision, by a 6-to-3 vote and written by Chief Justice Warren E. Burger, reversed a ruling by the Wisconsin Supreme Court, which had based its ruling on what it thought an earlier high court decision required.

Albert Shanker, president of the American Federation of Teachers, criticized the ruling in a statement this afternoon. He contended that the decision "strikes at the rights of all teachers and all public employees."

"The decision says that a school board may act as both judge and jury against employees who exercise their democratic rights as trade unionists," he added. "By declaring that the school board's hearing in the case represented impartial consideration of the facts, the Court flies in the face of common sense and political reality."

The Court's decision on the Miranda issue came in two companion cases from Ohio, involving the convictions of two men in state court on charges of selling marijuana. At the trial, the men contended that they were framed by a police informer. The prosecutor, in cross-examining them, repeatedly brought out the fact that neither of the defendants had given this account at the time of their arrest.

The state contended that necessity justified this practice: The discrepancy between the exculpatory story at the trial and the lack of any story at their arrest suggests that the story was fabricated along the way, according to the state, and unless the prosecutor could bring out this discrepancy at the trial, he would have little means of rebutting the exculpatory story.

SIMILAR ARGUMENT REJECTED

The Supreme Court rejected a similar argument last year, in a case involving cross-examination relating to "silence" in a Federal court trial. The Court reasoned then that the fact that the defendant had been silent at arrest did not have substantial probative value.

In that case, the Court acted on nonconstitutional grounds in its "supervisory" capacity in the Federal court system. It left open the question of constitutionality decided today.

In today's ruling, the Court cited its decision last year regarding the limited probative value of such testimony. Then it went on to note that the Miranda warnings gave the implicit assurance that silence would not be penalized.

"In such circumstances," the Court said, "it would be fundamentally unfair and a deprivation of due process to allow the arrested person's silence to be used to impeach an explanation subsequently offered at trial."

The dissent, by Justice Stevens and joined by Associate Justices Harry A. Blackmun and William H. Rehnquist, said that if the defendants had in fact been framed, their failure to say this at their arrest was "almost inexplicable."

'REASONABLE' DISMISSAL

In the Wisconsin case, the teachers had said state law required that dismissal of teachers be "reasonable." However, if the board were evaluating the reasonableness of dismissal as a remedy in this case, the teachers contended, the board would necessarily be evaluating its own conduct regarding the collective bargaining negotiations. Thus, it would not be impartial.

The Wisconsin court agreed, and ruled that due process required an impartial decisionmaker. It relied on a 1972 Supreme Court ruling on the need for impartiality in deciding parole revocation cases.

The Court majority, in reversing this, assumed that under state law the board was wholly free to make a policy judgment involving its assessment of the school system's best interests. The three dissenters appeared to suggest that if this assumption was accurate, they would agree there was no due process violation. They contended, though, that the decision should be sent back to the lower court to determine what the law was.

Due Process Under Review

REVIEW | BY TELFORD TAYLOR | MARCH 16, 1980

Democracy and Distrust
A Theory of Judicial Review
By John Hurt Ely.
268pp. Cambridge, Mass. Harvard University Press. $15.

IN 1897, REFLECTING growing public concern about dangerous and unhealthful employment, the New York State legislature enacted a statute limiting employment in bakeries to 60 hours a week. Four years later Joseph Lochner, a bakery owner, was convicted of violating the statute by permitting his employees to work longer than the specified maximum, and was fined $50. Lochner's lawyers, contending that the law was unconstitutional, carried his case all the way to the Supreme Court of the United States.

In 1905, in a famous (or infamous) decision, the Court held that the New York statute infringed Lochner's freedom of contract and was therefore unconstitutional under the clause of the 14th Amendment to the Constitution, which provides that: "No state shall make or enforce any law which shall ... deprive any person of life, liberty, or property without due process of law." Four members of the Court dissented, including Justice Oliver Wendell Holmes, who wrote that the Constitution was "not intended to embody a particular economic theory" and that the Court's decision "perverted" the meaning of the word "liberty" in the 14th Amendment.

Thereafter the name Lochner became the label for a series of Supreme Court decisions from 1905 to 1936 in which Federal and state socio-economic legislation was invalidated under what are known as the "due process" clauses of the Fifth and 14th Amendments. Political pressures raised by the economic depression of the 1930's, together with changes in the Court's membership, resulted in a series of decisions, beginning in 1937, which repudiated Lochner and its progeny.

Socio-economic legislation characteristic of the New Deal era was upheld by the Court, and it became the accepted view in legal circles that the proper office of the "due process" clauses was to ensure fair procedure in the imposition of regulatory restrictions or criminal penalties and that "due process" was not the source of substantive rights. "Substantive due process," as lawyers called the theory of the Lochner case, was sent to the doghouse.

But it would not stay there. The First Amendment itself limits only the Federal Government, but the Court continued to hold that the Amendment's guaranties of freedom of speech, press and religion are part of the "liberty" that the due process clause of the 14th Amendment forbids the states to infringe. Sexual lifestyles changed; contraception and abortion became respectable. Could Connecticut make the use of contraceptives a criminal offense? In 1965 the Supreme Court said no; but, except for Justice Harlan, the Justices still recoiled from relying on "substantive due process" and rested instead on "penumbras" emanating from a number of other constitutional provisions, in an opinion widely regarded as opaque.

Then in 1973 the Court heard constitutional attacks on state statutes making criminal the procurement or performance of abortions. In a case entitled Roe v. Wade the Court invalidated these statutes and, in so doing, for the first time since 1936, relied squarely and solely on "the 14th Amendment's concept of personal liberty." Substantive due process *redivivus*!

Now, the Constitution nowhere, explicitly or implicitly, says either that states may not limit the hours of labor in bakeries or ban the use of contraceptives or the performance of abortions, if, as most people still think, it was beyond the Court's proper function of constitutional interpretation — that it was "judicial legislation" — to invalidate New York's bakery labor law, is it not equally improper for the Court to tell the states what they may or may not do about contraceptives and abortions?

This is a basic constitutional problem, and it is one to which everyone can relate. There is today no more important constitutional question, and it is the question with which Prof. John Ely of the Harvard Law School deals in this rigorous, perceptive and very well-written book.

As a good democrat — small d — Professor Ely believes that laws should be written by elected legislators, not by life-appointed Federal judges and justices. Thus he rejects the idea that "due process liberty" vests the Court with a license to shut down state (or Federal) laws for other than procedural reasons. He contests the view of departed Justices such as Cardozo, Frankfurter and Harlan (now embraced by a majority of the present Court) that the substantive content of "liberty" can be derived from "tradition," the "teachings of history," "recognition of the basic values that underlie our society," "natural law," "privacy" or "consensus." Such phrases, he declares, are too vague to serve as limiting standards and operate rather to camouflage the Justices' reliance on their own predilections. That, of course, is undemocratic, and that is just what happened in Lochner and Roe v. Wade, both of which the author deplores.

Professor Ely divides the constitutional arena into "interpretivism" (constitutional decisions must be based on explicit or implicit textual meaning) and "noninterpretivism" (such decisions may he based on norms extraneous to the text but made applicable through general phrases such as "due process" and "liberty"). But he declares this to be "a false dichotomy," by which he means that other views are possible and, indeed, preferable.

Thus, despite Professor Ely's expressed admiration for the late Justice Hugo Black — the "quintessential interpretivist" — he rejects Black's view that the Bill of Rights (the first eight Amendments) are a complete catalogue of the guaranties made applicable to the states by the 14th Amendment. The reason is that Ely finds other constitutional provisions — in particular the Ninth Amendment and the "privileges and immunities" clause of the 14th Amendment — which, he believes, recognize additional particular unspecified norms, the substance of which must be found outside the text of the Constitution itself.

How to establish the qualities and boundaries of these unspecified norms so as to avoid the vice of vagueness, which, in Professor Ely's view, fatally infects substantive due process? Like Prof. Louis Lusky, who tackled a comparable problem in his book "By What Right" (1975), Professor Ely leans heavily on a famous (among lawyers) passage in an opinion written by Justice Harlan Eiske Stone in 1938 in which Stone spoke of the need for careful constitutional scrutiny of "legislation which restricts those political processes which can ordinarily be expected to bring about repeal of undesirable legislation" or which are "directed at particular religious or national or racial minorities."

On this footing Professor Ely erects a general standard that limits the unspecified norms to those which assist the functioning of representative democracy by "clearing the channels of political change" (into which category the First Amendment decisions readily fit), and by "facilitating the representation of minorities" (for which purpose the "equal protection" clause is particularly apt).

If not wholly original with Professor Ely, this thesis is developed in his book with a remarkable power of example and analysis. To be sure, it will not please every reader or completely satisfy any reader, but it is certain that no conceivable treatment of the problem would be received today with anything approaching general agreement.

Apart from the underlying theme, there are details in the analysis that are bound to trouble many readers (including this reviewer). As applied by the author, his tests would constitutionally validate laws exempting women from the draft or from the obligation to pay alimony. Neither has Professor Ely any constitutional objection to laws prohibiting the teaching of specific subjects, such as biology (shades of the Scopes "monkey law" trial!).

Professor Ely presupposes a pretty high intellectual and informational level on the part of the reader. At times his thought is necessarily intricate, and comprehension demands concentration. But it is a fine book, the reader's effort is well worthwhile, and the task is eased by Professor Ely's rare and delightful style — wry, witty and endowed with both dignity and informality. Would that more lawyers (including judges) could write half so well.

TELFORD TAYLOR is the author of "Munich: The Price of Peace," winner of the National Book Critics Circle nonfiction award for 1979.

High Court Rules on Rights of Aliens

SPECIAL TO THE NEW YORK TIMES | NOV. 16, 1982

Justices uphold a statutory act but then return the case on constitutional grounds.

WASHINGTON, NOV. 15 — The Supreme Court ruled today that a resident alien who leaves the United States briefly and tries to return may be barred from entry without full procedural protections to which aliens are entitled before they can be deported.

But the Court held unanimously that the exclusion procedure, however abbreviated, must comport with the constitutional requirements of due process.

The decision, the first full opinion of the term that began six weeks ago, was in most respects a victory for the Federal Government. The Justice Department had appealed a ruling by the Federal appeals court in California that an alien whose right to reenter the United States is in doubt must first be admitted and later given a full-dress deportation hearing. That process includes extensive rights to appeal and would, the Government argued, permit many aliens to abscond and avoid deportation altogether.

Writing for the Court today, Associate Justice Sandra Day O'Connor said Congress intended that an alien detained at the border receive only the less extensive exclusion hearing.

However, Justice O'Connor said, that hearing must "meet the essential standard of fairness under the due process clause." The Justice Department had conceded that due process guarantees such as adequate notice of the charges and a right to be represented by a lawyer did apply to the exclusion hearing. The department argued that the procedures in the case before the Court had met the constitutional standard.

Justice O'Connor said that the Court lacked sufficient evidence to decide whether the alien's constitutional rights had been adequately protected. Among the questions she raised was whether notice of less than 11 hours before the exclusion hearing was adequate.

The Court therefore sent the case, Landon v. Plasencia (No. 81-129), back to the United States Court of Appeals for the Ninth Circuit with instructions to decide the constitutional adequacy of the hearing that the alien received. Associate Justice Thurgood Marshall dissented from that part of the opinion, writing that the Supreme Court had adequate evidence to conclude that the alien had not received due process.

The ruling involved an alien who had previously been legally admitted to the United States. It does not apply to an alien seeking initial entry who, Justice O'Connor noted in passing, "has no constitutional rights regarding his application, for the power to admit or exclude aliens is a sovereign prerogative."

The alien in the case, Maria Plasencia, is a citizen of El Salvador who was living in Los Angeles. She made a brief visit to Mexico and was stopped at the border on the way back when immigration officials found six illegal aliens in her car.

Court Assails Holding of 2 for Year Without Trial

BY ARNOLD H. LUBASCH | NOV. 30, 1986

A FEDERAL JUDGE has been ordered to set conditions to release two men held without bail for more than a year on charges involving a major Wells Fargo robbery in Connecticut.

In ordering a hearing to set "reasonable conditions," the United States Court of Appeals for the Second Circuit ruled that holding the men any longer without a trial would "exceed even the flexible standards of due process."

In accordance with the decision, limiting pretrial detention under the Federal Bail Reform Act, the release hearing is to be held on Wednesday by Judge T. Emmet Clarie in Federal District Court in Hartford.

Stanley A. Twardy Jr., the United States Attorney in Connecticut, said on Friday that the Government would go forward with the hearing, rather than seek a review by the Supreme Court of the United States.

AN IMPORTANT ISSUE

The hearing concerns two defendants, Orlando Gonzales Claudio and Isaac Camacho-Negron, who are accused of transporting stolen money from the $7.6 million robbery of a Wells Fargo depot in West Hartford in 1983.

"Responsibility for the robbery," the appeals court noted, "has been claimed by a group calling itself Los Macheteros (the machete wielders), a paramilitary terrorist organization dedicated to achieving independence for Puerto Rico."

Judge Jon O. Newman wrote the decision for the appeals court, with the concurrence of Judge George C. Pratt and Judge Ellsworth A. Van Graafeiland. The 25-page ruling, issued Nov. 20 in Manhattan, directed Judge Clarie to set "reasonable conditions of release."

"This appeal," Judge Newman said, "presents the important issue of whether, and under what circumstances, the duration of the pretrial detention of a defendant denied bail because he is a risk to flee exceeds the limitations of the Due Process Clause of the Fifth Amendment."

The men who appealed their detention have been in jail since Aug. 30, 1985. Judge Clarie is detaining them under the Bail Reform Act because of a risk that they would flee. Their trial is expected to begin March 3 and to take about eight months to complete.

DETENTION 'UNCONSTITUTIONAL'

If the estimated time is correct, the appeals court observed, the two men will have been held for two years and two months before a "determination of their guilt or innocence."

"Without determining a single time period that marks the constitutional limit of pretrial detention in all cases," it added, "we conclude that the continued pretrial detention of these defendants, under the circumstances of this case, is unconstitutional."

The men in the appeal are among 20 defendants charged in connection with the Wells Fargo robbery. Some of them are also held without bail and are expected to press for release.

The appeals court said it agreed that the due process limit on the duration of preventive detention should be reviewed on a case-by-case basis. Various factors must be considered, it said, but eventually "the length of confinement would exceed constitutional limits regardless of the circumstances."

In the present case, it said, the Government was responsible for part of the trial delay, which added "considerable weight" to the argument for release. The men have been identified as members of Los Macheteros, which has been accused of bombings and other acts of violence in Puerto Rico.

Judge Newman said the appeals court recognized that "the release of these defendants upon reasonable conditions creates a risk that they may flee."

“The risk is serious,” he said, “but of at least equal gravity is the preventive detention for 14 months of defendants who are presumed innocent and whose trial to determine guilt or innocence will not even begin until detention has lasted 18 months.

“In mandating fundamental fairness, the Due Process Clause endeavors to set outer limits at which risks to society must be accepted to avoid unconscionable deprivations of the liberty of individuals.”

High Court Still Groping to Define Due Process

BY LINDA GREENHOUSE | MAY 31, 1990

WASHINGTON, MAY 30 — At first glance, the obscure divorce case the Supreme Court decided this week might have fit more comfortably on daytime television than on the Court's docket.

A New Jersey man made a brief visit to the California home of his estranged wife, where she surprised him by serving him with divorce papers. Was his fleeting presence in the state sufficient to subject him to the jurisdiction of the California courts? All nine Justices, rejecting the husband's constitutional arguments, agreed that it was, permitting the divorce suit to proceed.

The Court's current term, now entering its final month, is bound to produce more famous cases, more sweeping rulings, more dramatic results than this little-noticed decision. But as a window on the most fundamental constitutional debate now taking place within the Court, it would be hard to top Burnham v. Superior Court of California.

Underlying this dispute over jurisdiction was a profound question at the heart of the Court's institutional role: how to decide what interests the Constitution protects.

This question arises in contexts that are almost limitless, from the death penalty (Is it cruel and unusual punishment to execute murderers who are retarded?) to affirmative action (Do government preferences for blacks violate the equal protection rights of whites?). On many constitutional issues, a majority of the increasingly conservative Court has coalesced around a consistent approach, a set of shared premises, even if the outcome of individual cases is not entirely predictable.

But the Justices have yet to find a center of gravity in perhaps the most important constitutional context of all, the due process guarantee of the Fifth and 14th Amendments. That is the message of the case this week.

The husband's argument was that his contacts with California were so insubstantial and inadvertent that to subject him to the state courts' jurisdiction would deprive him of due process of law. While every Justice rejected this argument, they did so in four separate, very different opinions. No approach commanded a majority, demonstrating that the Court is much in flux in deciding what process is due under the Constitution.

The polar positions were taken by Justices Antonin Scalia and William J. Brennan Jr. Justice Scalia, writing for himself, Chief Justice William H. Rehnquist and Justices Byron R. White and Anthony M. Kennedy, surveyed the history of the law of personal jurisdiction. Justice Scalia said that in 1868, when the 14th Amendment was adopted, state courts were almost universally of the view that a person's physical presence, for whatever reason and however brief a time, was sufficient for jurisdiction.

"The short of the matter is that jurisdiction based on physical presence alone constitutes due process because it is one of the continuing traditions of our legal system," Justice Scalia said, adding, "Its validation is its pedigree."

Justice Brennan said that historical pedigree, while important, is not enough for deciding whether a particular governmental practice is consistent with due process. "All rules of jurisdiction, even ancient ones, must satisfy contemporary notions of due process," he said.

His opinion was joined by Justices Thurgood Marshall, Harry A. Blackmun and, significantly, Sandra Day O'Connor. Although usually a member of the Court's conservative majority, Justice O'Connor has expressed unease in the past with Justice Scalia's approach to due process, most notably in a case a year ago in which Justices Scalia and Brennan conducted a similar debate for a fractured Court.

The Justices themselves acknowledge that much more is at stake in these cases than illegitimacy or divorce jurisdiction. Justice Brennan said in this week's case that Justice Scalia's approach would foreclose the "evolution of our legal system." Justice Scalia replied that "the

American people," not "Justices of this Court," should control the pace of legal change. Consensus will remain elusive precisely because this debate matters so much.

Due Process Found to Apply Even in Temporary Holds on Property

BY LINDA GREENHOUSE | JUNE 7, 1991

WASHINGTON, JUNE 6 — The Supreme Court ruled today that states must provide a hearing before permitting a plaintiff in a private lawsuit to place a lien on the other side's property.

State courts commonly authorize liens of this type, which in effect turn the defendant's real estate into collateral against an eventual order to pay damages to the plaintiff.

The unanimous decision today declared unconstitutional a law in Connecticut, one of the few states that permit the procedure without giving the defendant advance notice and a chance to contest the judgment.

The ruling was based on the 14th Amendment's guarantee of due process. In an opinion by Justice Byron R. White, the Court said that the Connecticut law presented a serious risk of the "erroneous deprivation" of the defendant's rights.

BREADTH OF DUE PROCESS

"Our cases show that even the temporary or partial impairments to property rights that attachments, liens and similar encumbrances entail are sufficient to merit due process protection," Justice White said.

The decision, Connecticut v. Doehr, No. 90-143, upheld a ruling last year by the United States Court of Appeals for the Second Circuit, in New York. The state appealed and defended its law in the Supreme Court.

The state argued that the law provided adequate safeguards against mistakes and placed only an insignificant burden on the property owners, who retained possession of their property and could promptly contest the lien at a hearing after the fact.

WALLY MCNAMEE/CORBIS HISTORICAL/GETTY IMAGES

The Supreme Court ruled that a person is owed the due process of a hearing before there can be even a temporary hold on that person's property. Justice Byron R. White (front row, second from left) wrote the court's opinion in the case.

The state was joined by the Connecticut Bankers Association and the Savings Banks Association of Connecticut, which argued that the lien procedure was needed to insure the collection of hundreds of millions of dollars in defaulted real estate loans.

HARM TO CREDIT RATING

But Justice White's opinion stressed the harm that could befall defendants when liens were placed on their property without adequate justification. He noted that the lien, technically known as a "prejudgment attachment," could taint the property owner's credit rating and places a cloud on the title to the property, making it difficult to buy or sell.

Of 49 states — all except Pennsylvania — that provide for prejudgment attachment in at least some circumstances, only Connecticut, Washington and Rhode Island do not require prior hearings in routine cases. Twenty-seven states authorize prejudgment attachments only in extraordinary circumstances that make it necessary to secure the property.

Under the Connecticut law, a judge had to be persuaded before authorizing the lien that there was "probable cause" that the plaintiff would win the lawsuit. But Justice White noted that the law's definition of probable cause "remains obscure" and appeared to permit the judge in effect to take the plaintiff's word for essential facts about the lawsuit.

"The potential for unwarranted attachment in these situations is self-evident and too great to satisfy the requirements of due process absent any countervailing consideration," Justice White said.

The opinion said that one "countervailing consideration" might be evidence that the defendant was about to sell or transfer the property in order to avoid an eventual judgment. But there was no such indication in this case, Justice White said.

LIEN APPLIED AFTER FISTFIGHT

The case began in 1988 as a suit for injuries from a fistfight. The plaintiff, who said he had been "willfully, wantonly and maliciously assaulted" by the defendant, applied to a state Superior Court judge for a $75,000 lien on the defendant's house.

The defendant did not know that the order had been issued, or even that the lawsuit had been filed, until he got a notice from the county sheriff four days later. He then brought his own lawsuit in Federal District Court, challenging the attachment law as unconstitutional. He lost in the District Court before winning on appeal.

The Supreme Court has analyzed the Constitution's due process guarantee many times in order to decide the validity of laws authorizing the Government and private citizens to take someone else's property. The results have been confusing. For example, the Court has required hearings before a state can cut off welfare benefits, but not before the Federal Government can cut off Social Security disability benefits. It struck down a state law permitting creditors to garnishee a debtor's wages without advance notice or a hearing.

In a concurring opinion today, Chief Justice William H. Rehnquist and Justice Harry A. Blackmun said that the ruling "breaks new ground" by finding a due process violation in a procedure that does not actually amount to a "physical seizure" of assets. "Today's holding is a significant development in the law," the two Justices said.

In a second decision today, the Court upheld the imposition of $997,000 of sanctions against a Louisiana businessman for taking fraudulent legal positions and harassing the opposing party in a breach of contract suit over the ownership of a television station.

The 5-to-4 opinion, also written by Justice White, upheld a ruling by the United States Court of Appeals for the Fifth Circuit, in New Orleans. The appeals court, in turn, had upheld an action by a Federal District Judge in Louisiana, Nauman S. Scott, who also ordered the man's lawyers disbarred or suspended from practice. The amount of the fine was calculated to reimburse the other side for its lawyer's fees and other expenses.

The question in the case, Chambers v. NASCO Inc., No. 90-256, was whether Federal courts have the "inherent" power to punish fraudulent or bad-faith litigation, or whether their authority is defined by the Federal laws and procedural rules that address these situations. The district judge relied on the court's inherent power after concluding that the rules did not go far enough for the serious misdeeds that had occurred.

Justice White's opinion was joined by Justices Blackmun, Thurgood Marshall, John Paul Stevens and Sandra Day O'Connor. Justice Anthony M. Kennedy dissented, saying that the decision unduly expanded the power of the Federal courts. Chief Justice Rehnquist and Justice David H. Souter joined his opinion, and Justice Antonin Scalia dissented separately.

In Search of the Source of the Right to Privacy

BY TAMAR LEWIN | SEPT. 14, 1991

THROUGHOUT JUDGE Clarence Thomas's confirmation hearings, abortion has been discussed as part of a fundamental right to privacy guaranteed by the 14th Amendment, as the Supreme Court declared it to be in Roe v. Wade 18 years ago.

But legally the question is far more complicated, for neither the 14th Amendment nor the Constitution as a whole ever explicitly mentions privacy.

And even those who argue most fervently that the Constitution should be read to guarantee a right to abortion differ somewhat on which portion of the Constitution that right most logically springs from.

The 14th Amendment says, in part, "No State shall make or enforce any law which shall abridge the privileges or immunities of citizens of the United States; nor shall any State deprive any person of life, liberty or property without due process of law; nor deny to any person within its jurisdiction the equal protection of the laws."

RESTRICTIONS ON ABORTION

Some lawyers, including Lynn Paltrow of the American Civil Liberties Union's Reproductive Freedom Project, say that restrictions on abortion violate the 14th Amendment because they are a direct infringment on a woman's liberty and on equal protection for women.

Others, including Laurence Tribe of Harvard Law School, say they prefer to think of restrictions on abortion as violating the amendment's "privileges or immunities" clause.

But the High Court has taken a somewhat different tack, finding that the 14th Amendment implies a fundamental right to privacy, including the right to choose an abortion.

The idea that the courts should recognize a right to privacy first gained currency in a Harvard Law Review article in 1890 by Samuel Warren and Louis D. Brandeis, who were outraged in their belief that the Warren family's privacy had been violated by society-page coverage. Their proposal, however, was to make the violation of privacy a tort, or civil wrong, having nothing to do with the Constitution.

STERILIZATION CASE CITED

Many legal experts consider a 1942 case involving forced sterilization, Skinner v. Oklahoma, the first in a line of Supreme Court rulings creating a constitutional right to privacy in a person's procreative decisions. Although the Skinner ruling never mentioned the word "privacy" in striking down an Oklahoma law allowing forced sterilization of "habitual criminals," Justice William O. Douglas, writing for the Court, said that the law attacked a "basic civil right" and that any criminal subject to it was "forever deprived a basic liberty."

But it was not until 1965 that the Court explicitly recognized a constitutional right to privacy, in Griswold v. Connecticut, a case involving the legality of distributing contraceptives to married people. In that case, Justice Douglas reviewed several rights that were not specifically mentioned in the Bill of Rights but, by implication, had already had been found to exist in previous cases.

Justice Douglas cited the First, Third, Fourth, Fifth and Ninth Amendments as the source of the right to privacy. But Justices Arthur J. Goldberg, John Marshall Harlan and Byron R. White, while concurring in the ruling that the Constitution guaranteed privacy, thought the right emanated from the 14th Amendment's guarantee that citizens will not be deprived of "life, liberty or property without due process of law."

In Eisenstadt v. Baird (1972), the Court extended the privacy right to unmarried people, striking down a Massachusetts law prohibiting the distribution of contraceptives to them.

"If the right of privacy means anything, it is the right of the individual, married or single, to be free from unwarranted governmental intrusion into matters so fundamentally affecting a person as the decision whether to bear or beget a child," the Court said. It was this pronouncement on which Judge Thomas was unsuccessfully asked to take a position in questioning on Thursday.

A year later, in Roe v. Wade, the Court extended the right of privacy to a woman's decision to have an abortion.

"This right of privacy," the Court said, "whether it be found in the 14th Amendment's concept of personal liberty and restrictions upon state action, as we feel it is, or, as the District Court determined, in the Ninth Amendment's reservation of rights to the people, is broad enough to encompass a woman's decision whether or not to terminate her pregnancy."

Justices Insist Notice Be Given in Drug-Case Property Seizures

BY LINDA GREENHOUSE | DEC. 14, 1993

WASHINGTON, DEC. 13 — The Supreme Court ruled today that the Government may not seize a house or other real estate that it suspects of having been used in a drug transaction without giving the owner notice and a chance to contest the seizure at a hearing.

The 5-to-4 decision, written by Justice Anthony M. Kennedy, was the latest indication of the Court's discomfort with the Government's aggressive use of its forfeiture authority.

The Court ruled that the Government deprived a convicted drug dealer of his constitutional right to due process of law by taking possession of his house in Keaau, Hawaii, while he was out of the country, without notifying him or giving him a chance to object. The seizure came more than four years after the conviction, and the homeowner, James D. Good, had already paid a fine and served a year in prison.

The decision was the third time this year that the Court has curbed the sweeping power the Government claimed for itself to seize assets of suspected drug dealers. The civil forfeiture laws apply even if the property's owner has never been convicted of a crime, as long as the Government shows probable cause to believe that the property itself was used in committing a drug felony.

Many states have similar forfeiture laws that are affected by the constitutional analysis today.

The decision applies only to real estate and not to more portable possessions. It resolved a procedural issue — whether a hearing must precede rather than follow the seizure — and not the merits of the seizure itself. In that sense, it was more limited than the Court's unanimous ruling last June that a forfeiture can be so disproportionate to the underlying crime that it violates the Eighth Amendment's prohibition against "excessive fines."

Nonetheless, Justice Kennedy's opinion repudiated the Government's constitutional arguments and, to some degree, its motivation. For example, Justice Kennedy cited a 1990 Justice Department memorandum urging Federal prosecutors to make "every effort" to increase the income from forfeitures as a reason that property owners need the protection of a hearing "to ensure the requisite neutrality that must inform all governmental decision-making."

DUE PROCESS AT ISSUE

The Government had argued that the Fifth Amendment's guarantee of due process does not apply at all to civil forfeiture. Because forfeiture serves a "law enforcement purpose," the Government said, the only constitutional requirement was that the seizure be "reasonable" within the meaning of the Fourth Amendment. That amendment, barring unreasonable search and seizure, sets the standards for obtaining search warrants, which require no notice to the person whose property is to be searched.

But Justice Kennedy said that the broader protections of the Fifth Amendment's due process guarantee also applied, because "here the Government seized property not to preserve evidence of wrongdoing, but to assert ownership and control over the property itself."

He continued: "Individual freedom finds tangible expression in property rights. At stake in this and many other forfeiture cases are the security and privacy of the home and those who take shelter within it."

Justice Kennedy's opinion, U.S. v. Good, No. 92-1180, was joined by Justices Harry A. Blackmun, John Paul Stevens, David H. Souter and Ruth Bader Ginsburg. Chief Justice William H. Rehnquist dissented, along with Justices Sandra Day O'Connor, Antonin Scalia and Clarence Thomas.

In his dissent, Justice Thomas sounded particularly torn, saying that he approved of the majority's emphasis on private property rights and shared its concern over the breadth of the forfeiture laws.

But Mr. Good's case was not an "appropriate" one for setting new constitutional limits, Justice Thomas said, because he was persuaded that Mr. Good's rights had not been violated. He noted that Mr. Good was convicted of a drug offense involving his house and so was on notice that the house was a likely target for forfeiture.

In his opinion, Justice Kennedy appeared to take issue with this analysis when he said that it "founders on a bedrock proposition: fair procedures are not confined to the innocent."

FOUR-YEAR LAG

Mr. Good, who had 89 pounds of marijuana in his house when the police searched it in 1985, was working in Nicaragua and renting out the house when the Government seized it more than four years later. The tenants were told to send their rent checks to the Federal marshal.

When Mr. Good learned what had happened, he challenged the forfeiture in Federal District Court in Hawaii. He lost in that court, but won in the United States Court of Appeals for the Ninth Circuit, in San Francisco. The Bush Administration appealed, and the Clinton Administration carried on with the appeal after the Supreme Court accepted the case last March.

The question of whether the due process clause applies to forfeitures had divided the lower Federal courts for several years. The Federal appeals court in New York ruled in 1989 that notice and the opportunity for a hearing are required before seizure of real estate. The Federal appeals court in Atlanta had ruled three years earlier that there was no such requirement.

The Supreme Court last discussed the due process guarantee in the forfeiture context in 1974, when it ruled that the Government could seize a yacht without giving the owner notice. Today, Justice Kennedy said that the analysis used in that decision did not apply to the seizure of a home, because while a yacht can disappear, "real property cannot abscond."

Civil Rights Slaying Raises Speedy-Trial Issue

BY ADAM NOSSITER | MAY 27, 1994

JACKSON, MISS. — It took 30 years, the demise of all-white juries and a sea change in racial attitudes to convict an elderly white supremacist, Byron De La Beckwith, of the 1963 murder here of Medgar Evers, the Mississippi N.A.A.C.P. field secretary and civil rights pioneer.

After two mistrials in 1964, in which juries deadlocked, and the dropping of charges against Mr. Beckwith in 1969, justice had at last been done in 1994. That, at least, was the sentiment among Mississippi's black citizens, some of its white citizens, Mr. Evers's widow, Myrlie, and prosecutors after Mr. Beckwith, still unrepentant at 73, was sentenced to life in prison on Feb. 5.

Like the prosecution of aging Nazi war criminals, the new case against Mr. Beckwith was intended to close a "gaping wound laid open in society," as prosecutor Bobby DeLaughter said in his closing argument to the jury in February. Besides, there is no statute of limitations for murder.

But the Beckwith case and its attendant public turmoil is not over. His lawyers have appealed to the State Supreme Court, raising a constitutional issue that has dogged the case since Mr. Beckwith was reindicted in December 1990: Is justice long delayed justice denied?

His lawyers argue, and many otherwise unsympathetic lawyers fear, that in the 26-year gap between the crime and the reindictment, Mr. Beckwith was denied due process and the right to a speedy trial under the Fifth and Sixth Amendments.

"In the 14 years that I've practiced, I've never had constitutional issues that were this serious, that to me were this clear-cut," said Merrida Coxwell, one of Mr. Beckwith's two court-appointed lawyers. "These issues are very important to even the most average citizen."

Important, too, to the possible prosecution of other unresolved murder cases from the same era, when all-white Mississippi juries refused to convict whites for killing blacks, or civil rights workers of any race, for that matter. There is no shortage of such cases in Mississippi: the Southern Poverty Law Center has recorded 15 from the 1950's and 1960's, more than in any other Southern state.

Legal scholars say the Beckwith case may be the oldest to be prosecuted in American jurisprudence. "There is something, to my knowledge, unique about this," said Jerold Israel, a law professor at the Universities of Michigan and Florida. "There is that tremendous lapse."

Actually, there were three lapses: five years between the mistrials and the dismissal of Mr. Beckwith's indictment in 1969; 21 years between the dismissal of the indictment and his reindictment in 1990, and 26 years between the 1964 mistrials and the reindictment.

The inherent constitutional issues have worried a host of legal scholars and practitioners. The Mississippi Supreme Court signaled its own concern two years ago, when a sharply divided court ruled 4 to 3 that Mr. Beckwith's new trial must go forward before the issues could be formally considered. "Beckwith's indictment, arrest and anticipated trial may raise serious and troubling constitutional questions," Justice Armis Hawkins wrote for the majority.

The Chief Justice at the time, Roy Noble Lee, was more blunt. Prosecuting Mr. Beckwith, he said, would be an "egregious miscarriage of justice."

In a recent interview, Lloyd Weinreb, a professor at Harvard Law School, explained, "Whether you call it the right to a speedy trial or due process, it's going to come down to whether he can get a fair trial."

Critical to Mr. Beckwith's appeal on the speedy-trial ground is whether prosecutors intentionally or negligently allowed so many years to pass before they reindicted him.

Writing in a 1992 drug case, Doggett v. United States, in which six years passed between an indictment and trial, the United States Supreme Court said, "Excessive delay presumptively compromises the reliability of a trial." The Court added that negligence, as against bad faith, "still falls on the wrong side of the divide between acceptable and unacceptable reasons for delaying a criminal prosecution once it has begun."

But prosecutors argue from a 1982 Supreme Court decision that a speedy-trial claim can be invoked only if charges were pending against the defendant during the time in question. They were not in Mr. Beckwith's case, prosecutors say, recalling that the original indictment was dismissed in 1969.

That still leaves the argument that Mr. Beckwith's right to due process was violated. State and Federal precedent insist on two tests in establishing this claim: that the state deliberately delayed its case to gain an advantage, and that the defense was harmed by the long passage of years.

Prosecutors maintained that only Mississippi's transformed climate would permit a fair trial. Mr. DeLaughter, the assistant district attorney, wrote in his brief to the Mississippi Supreme Court: "Unlike one accused, who may move for a change of venue if he believes he cannot receive a fair trial at the place the crime occurred, the prosecution may only wait for passions about a case to subside. The prosecution did not attempt a third trial after the second mistrial because it was not possible to obtain a fair one."

MISSING BULLET

But the passing years that have allowed passions to cool have also allowed witnesses and memories to fade, Mr. Beckwith says, noting that only one of his three original lawyers is alive, and that lawyer is in his 80's; moreover, none of the lawyers preserved their files. The bullet that killed Mr. Evers is missing, Mr. Beckwith says, and many witnesses are dead and thus no longer available for cross examination, including the man who traded a telescopic gun sight to him; a man who provided him with an alibi, and a taxi driver who said that Mr. Beckwith had asked for directions to Mr. Evers's house.

Under well-established precedent, prosecutors were able to read a transcript of these witnesses' testimony into the record at the new trial. But Mr. Beckwith's lawyers could not cross-examine these witnesses — a severe disadvantage, he says, now that they have old police reports suggesting that the taxi driver was confused about the physical characteristics of the man who had asked him for directions. Since there is no transcript of the second mistrial, he added, there is no way of knowing whether witnesses who are now dead contradicted themselves.

Prosecutors argue that since two of Mr. Beckwith's alibi witnesses are alive, his defense was not critically damaged. As for the dead or missing, they said in their 1992 brief, "it's a two-edged sword" that cuts both the defense and the prosecution. There is nothing to suggest that evidence became lost because of "bad faith" on the state's part, they say.

Mississippians have "decided that mere lip service would not be paid to the law that imposes no statute of limitations for murder," Mr. DeLaughter wrote in his brief two years ago, "and that those guilty of assassinating political figures for their beliefs or through racial hatred would not go unpunished even after 20-plus years." The State Supreme Court will now balance that argument, which is central to efforts to resolve historic crimes, against the rights of those presumed to have committed them.

Inmate on Release Program Deserves Due Process, High Court Says

BY LINDA GREENHOUSE | MARCH 19, 1997

WASHINGTON, MARCH 18 — The Supreme Court ruled today that the State of Oklahoma had violated the due process rights of a convicted murderer when, without a hearing and on fewer than five hours' notice, prison officials ordered him back to prison after months of trouble-free freedom under an early release program.

In a unanimous opinion by Justice Clarence Thomas, the Court held that an inmate who has been released under a program to relieve prison crowding cannot be reincarcerated without getting a chance to show at a hearing that he has met the conditions of the program and is entitled to remain free.

The decision upheld a 1995 ruling by the United States Court of Appeals for the 10th Circuit, in Denver. Agreeing with the appeals court, the Justices rejected Oklahoma's argument that because an inmate on an early release program remains under the prison system's supervision, revoking the release is simply a change in the conditions of confinement, which does not invoke the protections of the 14th Amendment's due process guarantee.

The Supreme Court has ruled that an inmate is not entitled to a hearing before a transfer from a low-security prison to higher-security one.

Justice Thomas said the relevant analogy was not to a transfer from one prison to another, but to parole, which under a 1972 Supreme Court precedent cannot be revoked without a hearing. That decision, Morrissey v. Brewer, held that a revocation of parole was a "grievous loss" of liberty that inmates had a right to challenge in a formal proceeding.

Oklahoma's early release program, which, like programs in a dozen other states, is governed by a formula requiring the release of a certain number of prisoners as the prison system approaches capacity, "differed from parole in name alone," Justice Thomas said. Inmates in the program live on their own and are expected to get jobs and remain free of debt and out of trouble. They must report regularly to a parole officer and cannot leave the county without permission.

The inmate in this case, Ernest E. Harper, had followed the rules without incident when, at 5:30 on the morning of March 14, 1991, his parole officer called him and told him to report back to prison by 10 o'clock. The only reason given was that the Governor had denied his formal parole request, which had proceeded on a separate track unrelated to the early release program. Mr. Harper was given no hearing or chance to challenge the order, and he spent the next four years acting as his own lawyer while pleading his case to a series of state and Federal courts.

Mr. Harper, who had served 15 years of a life sentence when he won a place in the early release program in October 1990, was unsuccessful until the 10th Circuit's 1995 decision granting his petition for a writ of habeas corpus. The appeals court granted a stay of its order for Mr. Harper's release so the state could appeal to the Supreme Court.

Under today's decision, Young v. Harper, No. 95-1598, Mr. Harper will be released and will remain free unless the state can show at a hearing that he violated the terms of the program. It never alleged that he had committed any violations.

Today's decision was the second time in a month that the Supreme Court has ruled in favor of state prison inmates who were challenging their confinement by means of habeas corpus petitions in Federal court. Earlier, in Lynce v. Mathis, No. 95-7452, the Court ruled that Florida had violated the constitutional guarantee against ex post facto laws by retroactively revoking early release credits for a group of inmates.

Margaret Winter, a lawyer with the National Prison Project of the American Civil Liberties Union, whom the Court appointed to represent Mr. Harper in the case decided today, said in an interview that the decisions indicated that "it turns out there are limits" to the Court's often-expressed hostility to habeas corpus, and to its willingness to defer to state law-enforcement officials.

"The states are saying you can jerk people back into prison for any reason or no reason, and the Court said no," Ms. Winter said.

Ms. Winter said that Mr. Harper, who has only an eighth-grade education, had done such an impressive job of representing himself that she was surprised to learn, after the Supreme Court brought her into the case, that he had had no outside help.

In his opinion today, Justice Thomas expressed considerable impatience with Oklahoma's arguments, particularly with the state's effort to differentiate the early release program from traditional parole.

The Court also heard arguments today in a closely watched death penalty case from Virginia. The inmate, Joseph R. O'Dell 3d, is arguing that he was constitutionally entitled to inform members of the jury that sentenced him to death in 1988 that if given a life sentence, he would be ineligible for parole and so would not present a continuing danger to society.

The Supreme Court ruled in a 1994 case, Simmons v. South Carolina, that a capital defendant is entitled to such a jury instruction when the prosecution makes future dangerousness an issue. The question in the case today, O'Dell v. Netherland, No. 96-6867, is whether the 1994 ruling should be applied retroactively to cases like Mr. O'Dell's.

No Constitutional Right to Lie

EDITORIAL | BY THE NEW YORK TIMES | JAN. 24, 1998

THE SUPREME COURT took an appropriately dim view this week of the notion that government employees being investigated by their agencies for on-the-job misconduct have a broad, constitutionally protected right to lie. In a unanimous ruling, the Court overturned a Federal appeals court decision that barred Federal agencies from punishing employees for making false statements while denying an administrative charge of wrongdoing. The lower court cited concern about employees' due-process rights. But it was never clear how constitutional protection for untruthful responses would advance the due-process goal of avoiding unfair or inaccurate decisions by government.

"The core of due process is the right to notice and a meaningful opportunity to be heard," wrote Chief Justice William Rehnquist in the Court's terse opinion. "We reject, on the basis of precedent and principle, the view … that 'a meaningful opportunity to be heard' includes a right to make false statements with respect to the charged conduct."

Further, the decision noted, quoting from a 1969 Supreme Court decision, the nation's legal system "provides methods for challenging the Government's right to ask questions — lying is not one of them. A citizen may decline to answer the question, or answer it honestly, but he cannot with impunity knowingly and willfully answer with a falsehood."

CHAPTER 5

Due Process in the 21st Century

In the 21st century, after nearly every guarantee from the Bill of Rights had been extended to protect people from both state and federal infringement, the debate over due process became more about which people were entitled to these rights. Were poor defendants being set unreasonable bail? Could terrorist suspects — or migrants on the U.S.-Mexico border — be held indefinitely without a fair trial or even a preliminary hearing? These questions of how much due process was "due" in particular cases defied easy answers, as they intersected with issues of national security, immigration policy, gender and more.

Mocking Due Process

OPINION | BY BOB HERBERT | MARCH 14, 2002

I CALLED SHORN GREEN about 8:15 yesterday morning. He complained that I had awakened him.

I told him I wanted to talk about the murder of Danny Josephs.

"What's in it for me?" Mr. Green asked.

I said there was nothing in it for him, that I just wanted to hear what he had to say.

The murder happened in 1988. Mr. Green was one of two hard-core crack addicts whose testimony two years later sent a man named Lamont Branch to prison on a sentence of 25 years to life. Although Mr. Branch has served 13 years, he is almost certainly innocent. His older brother, Lorenzo Branch, has admitted shooting Danny Josephs, although he says the gun went off accidentally during a struggle.

Lorenzo is expected to repeat this, under oath, at a hearing in Brooklyn tomorrow. Lamont Branch's lawyer, Sara Bennett, hopes the hearing will lead to his release from prison.

The testimony of the crack addicts in 1990 was crucial. They both said they saw Lamont Branch and two others go into the victim's apartment on the morning of the shooting. And they said they heard shots. Their testimony was not just weak, it was embarrassing. Neither could remember when the shooting had taken place. One of the men, Thomas Edwards — who said he got high on crack about eight times every day — testified that Mr. Josephs had been killed in 1989. On cross-examination he acknowledged that he might have been off by a year or so.

When Shorn Green took the witness stand he was unable to remember what he had told cops about the shooting, or even when he had spoken to the police. He insisted that he had talked to investigators some time during the winter. He relented only after defense lawyers produced documents showing this had occurred in July 1989.

Both men testified that they had heard multiple shots. Mr. Edwards said there were two shots. Mr. Green said he heard three. There is no evidence showing that more than one shot was fired.

I called Mr. Green after reading a sworn affidavit — dated Oct. 10, 2001 — in which he declared that his "entire testimony was a lie." He told me he hadn't seen anything related to the killing of Danny Josephs. He said he hadn't been at the scene and he didn't know what had happened. He said he heard about the shooting from a friend.

When I asked why he had lied to the police, he said, "For money." He said Thomas Edwards had told him he would be paid if he told cops he saw Lorenzo Branch going into Mr. Josephs' apartment. He said he spoke to detectives on a number of occasions and each time he was given $20, which he spent on crack.

Neither addict could keep the story straight. In an extraordinary courtroom development, prosecutors pulled Mr. Edwards from the witness stand in the middle of his testimony when he offered information that hurt the prosecution's case. Mr. Edwards testified that he had seen Lamont Branch and two other men go into Mr. Josephs' apartment, and that one of the other men — not Mr. Branch — had a gun.

The assistant district attorney, over the vehement objections of the defense, interrupted the testimony and asked the court for permission to confer privately with her witness. Permission was granted. After the conference, Mr. Edwards once again took the witness stand. This time he said it was Lamont Branch whom he had seen with the gun. He said he had been too frightened to tell the truth the first time.

This is a ludicrous case. It mocks due process. It laughs at the idea that real and compelling evidence is required before a man can be taken into custody and sent off to prison for the better part of a lifetime.

What this case tells prosecutors is that all you need is a crack addict and a $20 bill.

Shorn Green now says that what he did was wrong and he regrets what happened to Lamont Branch. Lorenzo Branch, who has been saying for years that he was the shooter, is only now willing to testify in court about his culpability. "I am sorry," he said, "that it has taken me so long to completely come forward and take responsibility for what happened."

The Brooklyn district attorney, Charles Hynes, said yesterday that he was "open-minded" about the case. That is different from insisting that the right man is in prison.

"We need to hear what Lorenzo has to say," said Mr. Hynes.

BOB HERBERT is an Op-Ed columnist for The New York Times.

Court Appears Ready to Reverse a Sodomy Law

BY LINDA GREENHOUSE | MARCH 27, 2003

A MAJORITY OF the Supreme Court appeared ready today to overturn a Texas "homosexual conduct" law that criminalizes sexual practices between same-sex couples that are lawful in the state when performed by a man and a woman.

Texas is one of four states to make such a distinction, and one of 13 with criminal sodomy laws still on their books. It appeared from the argument today, on behalf of two Houston men who were prosecuted after the police found them having sex in a private apartment, that the court would follow a path of least resistance and invoke the constitutional guarantee of equal protection to strike down the Texas law.

A decision along those lines would sidestep the more fundamental question of the constitutional status of gay rights. But the fact that such a moment had arrived in a court that only 17 years ago dismissed as "facetious" the notion that the constitutional right to privacy extended to the private sexual choices made by gay men and lesbians invested the courtroom with an air of drama that the lopsided and unsuspenseful argument itself could not dispel.

It was a cultural as well as a constitutional moment, marked by the presence in the courtroom of many gay men and women from among the core of elite Washington lawyers. The seats in the center of the courtroom reserved for members of the Supreme Court bar were all claimed by 6:30 this morning for the 11 o'clock argument.

The argument proved to be a mismatch of advocates to a degree rarely seen at the court. Paul M. Smith, a former Supreme Court law clerk and experienced practitioner there, who argued for the two men, John G. Lawrence and Tyron Garner, was assured and elegant in his presentation. Mr. Smith was unperturbed even while sparring with

Justice Antonin Scalia, a predictable adversary whose vote he had no chance of winning and whose questions he was able at times to turn to his clients' advantage.

Charles A. Rosenthal Jr., the district attorney for Harris County, Tex., whose job was to defend the Texas law, was making his first Supreme Court argument, and he made a first-timer's mistakes. He appeared surprised by questions that more experienced lawyers would easily have anticipated and unable to recognize the helping hand that Justice Scalia regularly offered. The justices ended up talking over Mr. Rosenthal, sparring with one another.

Of the 35 questions that the justices asked Mr. Smith during his 30-minute argument — all except Justices John Paul Stevens and Clarence Thomas asked him at least one question — 23 came from Justice Scalia. The others appeared content to let the long colloquies between the two sharpen and showcase the issues.

For example, one of Mr. Smith's goals was clearly to persuade the court that while the concept of gay rights as such did not have deep historical roots, there was a libertarian spirit of personal privacy that did reach far back to the country's beginnings. "So you really have a tradition of respect for the privacy of couples in their home, going back to the founding," Mr. Smith said. He noted that three-quarters of the states had repealed their criminal sodomy laws for everyone, "based on a recognition that it's not consistent with our basic American values about the relationship between the individual and the state."

"Well, it depends on what you mean by our basic American values," Justice Scalia said, clearly unimpressed by the argument that a newly emerged consensus on any subject should receive constitutional weight. "Suppose that all the states had laws against flagpole sitting at one time" and subsequently repealed them, Justice Scalia said. "Does that make flagpole sitting a fundamental right?"

This gave Mr. Smith an opening, and he took it. "No, your honor," he said, "but the court's decisions don't look just at history, they look at the function that a particular claimed freedom plays in the lives of real people." He offered the rights to contraception and abortion as examples.

"I don't know what you mean by the function it plays in the lives of real people," Justice Scalia said. "Any law stops people from doing what they really want to do."

Mr. Smith replied, "The court has said that it's going to use reasoned judgment to identify a realm that involves matters central and core to how a person defines their own lives."

The case, Lawrence v. Texas, No. 02-102, is an appeal from a ruling by the Texas Court of Appeals, which upheld the law. In bringing the appeal, the Lambda Legal Defense and Education Fund attacked the law both on the basis of equal protection and due process, describing sexual intimacy in the home as an aspect of the "liberty" that the due process guarantee protects. The due process argument, the more far-reaching, would require the court to disavow its 1986 precedent, Bowers v. Hardwick, which upheld Georgia's sodomy law against a due process challenge.

Mr. Smith waited until near the end of his argument to address the 1986 precedent directly, prompted by a question from Justice Ruth Bader Ginsburg. He said the decision was based on faulty "assumptions that the court made in 1986 about the realities of gay lives and gay relationships." The court may not have known it then, he said, but "it has to be apparent to the court now that there are gay families, that family relationships are established, that there are hundreds of thousands of people registered in the 2000 Census who have formed gay families."

For this population, the right to privacy for sexual expression in their own homes "performs much the same function that it does in the marital context," he said, describing his basic argument as "that it doesn't make sense to draw a line there and that you should protect it for everyone."

Mr. Rosenthal had a basic argument to present as well. It was, he said, that "Texas has the right to set moral standards and can set bright-line moral standards for its people." He asked the court "not to disenfranchise 23 million Texans who ought to have the right to participate in questions having to do with moral issues."

Justice Stephen G. Breyer pressed Mr. Rosenthal to explain further. He quoted the old nursery rhyme: "I do not like thee, Dr. Fell / The reason why, I cannot tell," and asked Mr. Rosenthal how the state's position differed. Justice Breyer said at one point in frustration: "I would like to hear your straight answer to those points," the unintended double-entendre provoking a ripple of laughter in the courtroom.

Justice Sandra Day O'Connor, whose vote is the least predictable and consequently of the most interest in the case, asked only two questions, both to Mr. Smith. She seemed to be seeking assurance that the court need not issue a broad ruling in order to invalidate the Texas law.

Judge Steps In for Poor Inmates Without Justice

BY LESLIE EATON | MAY 23, 2006

NEW ORLEANS — Hurricane Katrina took his house, his courtroom and, Judge Arthur L. Hunter Jr. says, his faith in the way his city treats poor people facing criminal charges.

Nine months after the storm, more than a thousand jailed defendants have had no access to lawyers, the judge says, because the public defender system is desperately short of money and staffing, without a computer system or files or even a list of clients.

And so Judge Hunter, 46, a former New Orleans police officer, is moving to let some of the defendants without lawyers out of jail. He has suspended prosecutions in most cases involving public defenders. And, alone among a dozen criminal court judges, he has granted a petition to free a prisoner facing serious charges without counsel, and is considering others.

It is, he said in an interview, his duty under the Constitution. “Something needs to be done, it’s that simple,” he said. “I’m the lightning rod, yes.”

The district attorney’s office opposes letting defendants back out on the street, saying the court should find them lawyers. But Judge Hunter said he has had little luck finding private firms willing to take on most indigents’ cases, and there appears to be no money to pay their expenses.

The public defenders’ office, run not by City Hall but by a parish board, is basically broke. Louisiana, alone among the states, relies mainly on local court fees — mostly surcharges on traffic tickets — to finance its public defenders, according to the National Legal Aid and Defender Association.

It is a financing system that Judge Hunter and Calvin Johnson, the chief judge of the criminal court in New Orleans, have recently found to be unconstitutional because it forces poor people to pay for the system. The Louisiana attorney general's office says it plans to appeal those decisions.

In Orleans Parish, the traffic and the tickets both evaporated after Hurricane Katrina. Most of the office's 42 part-time public defenders were laid off. And they were, by many accounts, inadequate to begin with; a new study sponsored by the federal Justice Department says that the office probably needs 70 full-time lawyers, a computer system for case management, support staff and a reliable source of financing.

The study calls for scrapping the current system, which an appeals court decision recently described as "overburdened, underfunded and perhaps unconstitutional." The public defenders' office in New Orleans is slated to receive a $2.8 million federal grant on May 31 — but the study says it needs more than $10 million to get up and running and operate for a year.

The criminal justice system in New Orleans was notoriously troubled long before the storms, and if anything, it is now worse. Officials hope to resume jury trials soon for the first time since Hurricane Katrina, but still do not know if they will have enough courtrooms, jurors or witnesses to proceed.

On a recent Friday morning, in a borrowed courtroom in the Federal Building downtown, Judge Hunter listened to testimony from Ronald Dunn, 43, who was arrested on Aug. 19, 10 days before Hurricane Katrina hit, on a charge of possessing crack cocaine. Like the vast majority of the defendants in criminal court here, he cannot afford to hire a lawyer, and so would normally be represented by a public defender.

Handcuffed, shackled and wearing jailhouse orange, Mr. Dunn told the court that as the water rose, he spent four frightening days without food in the House of Detention, and was then moved from prison to prison, losing touch with his family.

In the nine months since the hurricane, he said, he has never even spoken to a lawyer. "I don't have a lawyer," Mr. Dunn said. "I never

OZIER MUHAMMED/THE NEW YORK TIMES

Judge Arthur L. Hunter Jr. has suspended criminal prosecutions in most cases involving public defenders in New Orleans.

been to court." Without a lawyer a defendant cannot even plead guilty.

Pamela R. Metzger, the director of the Criminal Court Clinic at Tulane Law School, has petitioned the court to release Mr. Dunn and more than a dozen other poor prisoners in similar circumstances. Releasing them would not hamper the prosecution, she argued, and would give them an opportunity to try to gather evidence in their own defense. And, she said later, "to be free from imprisonment and punishment without due process of law."

But David S. Pipes, an assistant district attorney, argued against releasing Mr. Dunn, whom he described as a five-time felon. (Court documents show that Mr. Dunn has been arrested 10 times since 1990 and has pleaded guilty to previous drug and theft charges.)

More broadly, Mr. Pipes said: "The proper solution for someone who does not have an attorney is to get them an attorney. Releasing them does not cure anything and does not protect their rights."

Of course, everyone in the courtroom could describe a life turned upside down by Hurricane Katrina. Mr. Pipes is working out of an office in an old nightclub because the district attorney's office flooded. Professor Metzger is commuting to New Orleans from Atlanta.

And Judge Hunter is driving back and forth to Tampa, Fla., where his family fled, or Baton Rouge, where he has bought a house where he plans to live with his wife and teenage son, a cousin and a widowed aunt.

Over the years, the district attorney and others have accused Judge Hunter of being too soft on defendants, and of having too high an acquittal rate in nonjury trials. (He says he is simply fair.) But even longtime critics like the independent Metropolitan Crime Commission say that when it comes to the public defenders' office, he is doing the right thing.

"I don't have any problem with what he's trying to do there," said Rafael C. Goyeneche III, president of the commission. "He's demanding that it function properly."

The battle over indigent defendants is proceeding on several levels. Last month, Judge Hunter granted a petition for release filed by Professor Metzger on behalf of Donald Crockett, a mentally ill man accused of being a felon in possession of a firearm. He has been in jail since October 2003.

The district attorney's office appealed, and an appellate court found that additional procedural steps were required. Though it reversed the judge's decision, the court suggested such releases might be possible once the program completely runs out of money. Professor Metzger said she planned to appeal to the Louisiana Supreme Court.

Gov. Kathleen Babineaux Blanco has submitted a budget that would double, to $20 million, the appropriation for defenders around the state, and a legislative task force set up before Hurricane Katrina continues to work on the issue.

The Louisiana State Bar Association has made fixing the public defender system a priority and has paid for both another study and for the salaries of three defenders for a year, said Frank X. Neuner, president of the bar association. In Orleans Parish, the criminal court judges have appointed new directors (including Professor Metzger) to oversee the public defenders' program.

Judge Johnson, who runs the criminal court and is a former public defender himself, has been working to build a consensus for changing the system, something he said he has supported for years. He was the first judge after Hurricane Katrina to order an investigation into whether the public defenders could adequately represent the poor.

But having Judge Hunter halt prosecutions and consider freeing inmates has helped focus attention on the issue, Judge Johnson said.

"You have to have some guy out there rattling the saber, absolutely," Judge Johnson said. "I think the message was loud, clear and necessary."

For Poor, Bail System Can Be an Obstacle to Freedom

BY JOHN ELIGON | JAN. 9, 2011

BEFORE GEORGE ZOUVELOS agrees to post someone's bail, a customer must put up cash, sign a 20-page contract and initial 86 separate paragraphs.

Those paragraphs are chock-full of fees: $250 if the defendant misses a weekly check-in; as much as $375 an hour for obscure tasks like bail consulting and research; and unspecified amounts if Mr. Zouvelos, a bail bondsman based in Manhattan, farms out tasks like obtaining court documents or delivering release papers to jail.

Then there are the thousands of dollars that Mr. Zouvelos can charge if he decides to revoke a bond and return a defendant to jail, as he did 89 times during a four-month period last year.

The common perception of how the bail-bond system operates is fairly straightforward: A bondsman bails a defendant out of jail. If that defendant misses a court appearance, the bondsman can "surrender" him — chase him down and haul him back to jail.

The reality is more troubling.

Vague laws and insufficient oversight have allowed some bondsmen in New York to return defendants to jail for questionable or unspecified reasons, and then withhold thousands of dollars to which they may not be entitled, according to lawyers, judges, state regulators and even some bondsmen.

Those cases turn the system on its head: Those who are supposed to give poor defendants a shot at freedom while their cases are pending are instead the ones locking them up and disenfranchising them further.

The laws "are open for exploitation," said James Carfora, a Long Island-based bail bondsman.

"They need to be more specific," he said. "If I bail a guy out today and I don't like him, I can put him back in jail, and it's O.K. To me, that's screwed up."

Complaints against bondsmen have risen in recent years, according to the New York State Insurance Department. Although the allegations may often involve only a thousand dollars, that sum can be the difference between freedom and detention for indigent defendants who make up most of bondsmen's clientele.

Over a four-year period that ended in mid-July, the department received 227 complaints against 43 bail-bond agents. But those figures may represent only a fraction of the actual grievances: People often do not know when a bondsman is violating their rights or where to file a complaint, experts say.

But the complaints have been alarming enough that the Insurance Department, which licenses bondsmen, is considering implementing new regulations intended to rein in agents who do things like place onerous restrictions on defendants, frequently surrender them, and deduct excessive fees from the cash collateral that clients are supposed to get back.

"Our current enforcement actions are more aggressive than in the past, but the regulations need to be enhanced to provide additional enforcement powers," said Steven Nachman, the head of the department's frauds and consumer services bureaus.

Justice Thomas A. Farber of State Supreme Court in Manhattan was so disturbed by the number of defendants that bondsmen were surrendering that he wrote a letter to the borough's administrative judge within the past year expressing his concern.

"It is a process and an industry that seems to elude effective regulation," said Timothy J. Murray, the executive director of the Pretrial Justice Institute, a Washington organization that advocates bail reform. "So much of the business transaction is not subject to the public view, nor to much in the way of scrutiny."

Bail is money that defendants give courts to hold in exchange for their freedom while their cases are pending. But thousands of defendants who lack the money to post bail turn to bondsmen, who charge a percentage of the bail amount and submit a bond to the court, promising to pay the bail if the defendant flees.

The bondsmen often take collateral — usually cash or property — that is supposed to be returned as long as a judge does not order the bail forfeited.

A more common complaint among defendants who pay the collateral in cash is that bondsmen keep some or all of it, deducting fees for unnecessary or invented services. Some bondsmen say the fees are for legitimate purposes like rearresting a defendant. For defendants who have been rearrested, the effects can be devastating: unless the collateral was returned, they often do not have enough money to pay for a new bond.

During a four-month period in 2010, Mr. Zouvelos sent back to jail at least 89 people whom he had bailed out, including some defendants who had not missed a single court appearance, said Vincent Conwell, one of Mr. Zouvelos's contract bounty hunters.

"I'd say 60 percent of the people I put back in jail I feel bad for putting them back," Mr. Conwell said. "You start thinking like, 'This guy really shouldn't be going back.' "

Mr. Zouvelos said his staff was now better at tracking cases, so he no longer had to surrender as many defendants.

The contract that Mr. Zouvelos requires customers to sign includes a charge of 15 percent of a client's bail amount if he rearrests the client — essentially giving himself a financial incentive to throw back in jail someone he has bailed out.

Mr. Zouvelos said a large part of the fees he charged went to vendors for things like locating, rearresting and transporting the clients. He said he did not keep any of the money.

He also defended his practice and the industry, saying that bail bondsmen take on a lot of financial risk and that he must do what he can to avoid having to pay the courts when his clients skip bail.

"By curtailing the activity and constantly monitoring the bonds," Mr. Zouvelos said, "it's mitigating loss. I take less collateral and give people a shot. Those are traditionally much riskier undertakings."

One of his clients, Annette George, said that in March, Mr. Zouvelos revoked her son's $15,000 bond and threw him back in jail. About two months earlier, she had given Mr. Zouvelos's company more than $5,000 in premium and collateral for her son, Travis Saunders, 20.

At a hearing in State Supreme Court in Manhattan the day after Mr. Saunders was sent back to jail, his lawyer said the bond company explained that it had surrendered Mr. Saunders because of new "police contact." But the judge, the prosecutor and the defense lawyer had no record of any new contact by the police with Mr. Saunders.

State laws do not require bondsmen to give a reason, and no one from Mr. Zouvelos's company was in court to explain. The judge kept Mr. Saunders in custody, setting a new bail of $3,500, and freeing Mr. Zouvelos from the bond.

Now, 10 months later, Ms. George said she still has not received the $4,150 in collateral she had given Mr. Zouvelos, and she has since sued him for it.

Mr. Zouvelos acknowledged that Ms. George's contract called for the collateral to be returned in 90 days, and he said he was not sure why she had not received it within that period. In any case, Mr. Zouvelos said, he was now holding on to the money because Ms. George might be responsible for paying his legal bills in what he characterized as her frivolous lawsuit.

Ms. George also broke Mr. Zouvelos's rules by filing a lawsuit, he said, because his contract stated that all disputes had to be settled through arbitration.

Since 2005, the Insurance Department has received about 60 complaints against Mr. Zouvelos and his company, Spartan Bail Bonds.

Last week, the department filed administrative charges against Mr. Zouvelos, saying among other things that he had charged improper fees and failed to return collateral and premium. The department has identified a dozen cases over a period of two and a half years in which Mr. Zouvelos received a total of more than $41,000 in collateral but returned only about $15,000 of it to clients. A hearing on the charges has been scheduled for next month.

JAMES ESTRIN/THE NEW YORK TIMES

Laws regulating bail bondsmen "are open for exploitation," said James Carfora, a bail-bond agent.

Mr. Nachman, the head of fraud and consumer services, declined to comment on specific cases, but he said it was generally difficult to determine what fees were improper because the law allowed bondsmen to enter into private contracts with the people they bail out. In Mr. Zouvelos's case, the department has charged that he acted in an untrustworthy and incompetent manner.

Mr. Zouvelos pleaded guilty last year to misdemeanor charges of possessing an unloaded shotgun and knife, and attempting to pass the weapons to someone else while the police were arresting him in his office. He was sentenced to 10 days of community service.

Another case in Manhattan illustrated how a bail-bond company could try to extract extra money from anyone associated with a bond.

In May, Affordable Bails, a company with seven offices in the New York area, posted a bond for Abdur Rashid Salaam, who had been arrested in Manhattan on grand larceny charges. Property and $5,000 were given as collateral on Mr. Salaam's behalf.

About a month later, Affordable Bails sent Mr. Salaam back to jail. Mr. Salaam's lawyer at the time, Gary G. Becker, said he had to argue with the company before it returned the $5,000, which Affordable Bails did not record on the bond affidavit filed in court, even though the law required that the collateral be listed.

When Affordable Bails returned the $5,000, an agent with the company demanded $10,000 in recovery fees from the two people whose signatures were on the bond: Mr. Salaam's daughter, Robinette Merritt, and a friend, James Greene. The bond company threatened them with jail, according to Ms. Merritt and Mr. Greene's former lawyer, Dawn Florio.

"I didn't understand what all these costs were for," Ms. Florio said, adding that Mr. Salaam "turned himself in" and "it wasn't like you had to go bounty hunting to get him."

Mr. Greene paid an additional $2,000, Ms. Florio said, and Affordable Bails stopped asking for more after she became involved.

Because Mr. Salaam had been surrendered, a judge set his new bail at $75,000, which Mr. Salaam has not posted. Lewis Lilla, an owner of Affordable Bails, declined to comment.

Mr. Becker wrote in an e-mail that he was troubled that "a defendant can be ordered imprisoned by a court based solely on the unsworn, untested word of a non-law-enforcement civilian, a civilian who stands to profit financially if the defendant is incarcerated." The lawyer added, "That is not due process of law."

Justice Michael J. Obus, the administrative judge in State Supreme Court in Manhattan, said he periodically received complaints from judges about seemingly improper bond revocations. But he said it was up to the department to respond to complaints of improper surrender.

"I really don't think we have much choice but to accept the defendant back if the bond company doesn't want to continue taking responsibility for it," Judge Obus said.

A Terror Trial, With or Without Due Process

OPINION | BY JEFFREY ROSEN | SEPT. 10, 2006

SOME DEBATES ARE SO polarized, with the competing sides so certain that any compromise would be dangerous, that it's hard to imagine any middle ground emerging.

The argument over how to try the 14 terror suspects recently transferred from Central Intelligence Agency prisons to military custody at Guantánamo Bay seems to be one of them.

On one side is the Bush administration, which last week proposed that these suspects, whom it called the most dangerous in the war on terror, should be tried in military commissions under procedures that the White House asked Congress to endorse.

Under the Bush proposal, the trials would not resemble any civilian trials or courts-martial held in the United States. Hearsay evidence and evidence obtained under coercion or duress could be admitted. And suspects could be denied access to classified evidence, although it would be disclosed to their military defense lawyers.

On the other side of this debate are civil libertarians who insist that suspected terrorists can't receive fair trials unless they are given the protections of an ordinary court-martial — including the right to exclude hearsay and coerced evidence and the right to see evidence against them.

So, what's a fair trial and how much due process does it require? Can the suspected terrorists be tried by a tribunal that lacks some of the protections that military defendants ordinarily demand? Surprisingly enough, this is not a debate about what the law requires. Short of endorsing cruel and unusual punishments for terrorists, Congress can set up whatever military commissions it likes.

"The administration's proposals, if adopted by Congress, would almost surely pass muster with the Supreme Court," said Peter Spiro, who teaches international law at Temple University. "Congress may not have complete carte blanche, but in the Hamdan case last June, four of the justices who voted against the commissions stressed that the president could always go back to Congress to get the authority he wanted."

The issue, then, is more about the court of public opinion: how a trial, without the customary procedural rights, would be perceived in the United States and abroad.

Inevitably, the military commissions, whatever form they take, will be compared to the Nuremberg trials in which Nazi war crime defendants were given due process — up to a point.

"At Nuremberg, there was no secret evidence and no closed proceedings that the defendants' counsel was excluded from, although it's not clear how much physical access to the evidence the individual defendants had," said John Barrett, who teaches at St. John's University law school. "Hearsay and evidence produced by coercive methods weren't formally excluded by the Nuremberg charter, but the American interrogators didn't do rough stuff like water boarding — although there might have been a corner or two cut that the coercion standard would find troubling."

Many want the United States to meet this Nuremberg standard, which they believe gave it authority and credibility over the next half century to serve as a global model of due process.

"The trials shouldn't differ fundamentally from the fair trial provisions in any trial, especially when you have the potential death penalty or life in prison," said Richard Goldstone, the South African chief prosecutor of the United Nations International Criminal Tribunals for the former Yugoslavia and Rwanda. "To exclude a defendant from any part of the trial, or to withhold evidence from the defendant, seems to me, by any civilized standard, outside what is acceptable."

He added, "The other objectionable provision is that evidence would be admitted even if obtained under duress or torture."

But other legal scholars say that this is a different time. For one thing, they point out, the war is not over. "In a war situation, international commissions often use hearsay as long as it's reliable," said Jack Goldsmith of Harvard Law School, who led the Office of Legal Counsel under President Bush.

Other scholars who defend the administration argue that national security cannot be compromised.

"The issue of access to classified information is pivotal," says John Yoo, who helped the Bush administration draft an earlier version of the proposed commissions and who now teaches law at University of California, Berkeley. In his new book, "War By Other Means," Professor Yoo argues that in the first World Trade Center bombing case in 1993, prosecutors had to give the defense a list of 200 unindicted co-conspirators. The list, he writes, was "delivered to bin Laden" and "was later found during the investigation of the African embassy bombings."

Republicans in Congress are now negotiating with the Bush administration on a series of compromises. The military commissions may operate closer to the Nuremberg standard, but give the administration some of the authority it seeks. For example, one proposal would allow the use of hearsay and evidence obtained through coercion short of torture, while refusing to allow the use of evidence not disclosed to the defendant.

Could this satisfy critics? Some legal scholars suggest that a trial conducted along these lines could have international legitimacy as well as meeting basic standards of due process. Even Mr. Goldstone, the chief prosecutor for the U.N. tribunals, says that jettisoning the use of secret evidence would remove the "most objectionable" part of the proposal.

Professor Spiro of Temple University agrees. "The Republican moderates' proposal would come a lot closer to satisfying international opinion, and in part because it's coming from the Senate and not the administration," he said.

Still, the atmospherics of the trial, and the fact that the defendants face the death penalty, may make it harder for the verdict to be internationally accepted.

"Guantánamo is now a rallying cry in Europe, so any trials that take place there will be tainted by that fact alone," Professor Spiro said. "The administration would be well advised to allow the proceedings to be televised to avoid the image of a show trial."

But televised proceedings might give the defendants a political platform to hijack the proceedings. "There's always a danger that this will degenerate into a political circus," says Professor Goldsmith. "Slobodan Milosevic used the trial against him as a political platform, and Saddam Hussein is doing the same thing. The more procedural rights you give the defendant, the more you allow him to continue the war by other means."

Professor Goldsmith says the debate about what a fair trial requires will continue throughout every stage of the terrorist trials — from the initial indictments to the actual trials to the Supreme Court appeals that would follow any death sentence. "There's a trade-off," he said. "You can clamp down on access, but you do so at the cost of the perception of fairness, and finding the right balance of fairness and control is very hard."

JEFFREY ROSEN's latest book is "The Most Democratic Branch: How the Courts Serve America."

Due Process, Bulldozed

OPINION | BY BOB HERBERT | SEPT. 25, 2006

UNTIL FIVE MONTHS AGO, Bilal Hussein was part of a team of Associated Press photographers that had won a Pulitzer Prize for photos documenting the fighting and carnage in Iraq.

Now he's a prisoner, having been seized by the U.S. government.

You might ask: What's he been charged with?

The answer: Nothing.

There was a flurry of interest last week in the case of Maher Arar, a terror suspect who was shipped to Syria and tortured before it was learned that, alas, he was not a terrorist. Mr. Hussein got a little news coverage last week, as well. People who still think there is a place in this world for fairness, justice and due process are calling on the authorities to either charge him with a crime or release him.

Mr. Hussein, an Iraqi hired by The A.P., was taken into custody by U.S. forces in Ramadi last April 12. As in many similar cases, U.S. officials have been saying — without disclosing evidence to back up their comments — that he had improper ties to the insurgents.

But neither the Americans nor the Iraqis have officially charged Mr. Hussein with anything.

Scott Horton, a prominent New York lawyer called in by The A.P. to work on the case, said: "The administration always starts with a broad-brush tarring of these individuals. You'll have officials saying: 'Oh, they're bad dudes. They're evil. We have evidence we can't show you that would demonstrate just how terrible these people are.'

"Well, sometimes they do. But very frequently, alarmingly frequently, they don't."

Mr. Hussein's case closely resembles that of Abdul Ameer Hussein, a cameraman hired by CBS News who was wounded while covering an attack on an American convoy in Mosul on April 5, 2005. He was shot by a U.S. soldier, a sniper who was more than 200 yards away.

Mr. Hussein was taken to a hospital. His camera and videotapes were seized. And despite his CBS press credentials, which were checked out and found to be legitimate, he was arrested by U.S. authorities and imprisoned. Much of his time over the course of the next year was spent in solitary confinement at the Abu Ghraib prison, where he was subjected to coercive interrogation and other indignities.

For what?

American officials were telling reporters, without offering any evidence, that Mr. Hussein had been collaborating with insurgents. He hadn't been. It turned out he was completely innocent. In fact, he was a kind of timid guy who was less than thrilled about having a job that required him to shoot combat footage.

This is a spooky time in history. It's one thing for tyrannical regimes like the old Soviet Union and Communist China to bulldoze the very idea of human rights and human decency by engaging in such atrocities as detention without trial, torture and other forms of state terror. It's something else completely when the United States, the greatest symbol of liberty that the world has ever known, begins to head down that hellish road.

Abdul Ameer Hussein ultimately was able to escape the clutches of the authorities because of the persistent legal effort pushed by CBS News on his behalf. Scott Horton was part of that effort. A year after he was taken into custody, Mr. Hussein, manacled and wearing an orange jumpsuit, was walked into a Baghdad courtroom for a trial. It was quickly determined that the case against him was ludicrous.

"There was absolutely no evidence against this guy," said Mr. Horton. "Even the attorney general of Iraq said there was no basis for proceeding against him."

The case was dismissed.

Several Iraqi journalists working for international news organizations have been held without charge by American and Iraqi forces. The absence of concrete evidence in so many of the cases is disturbing, to say the least.

"I am absolutely convinced," said Mr. Horton, "that the ton of bricks fell on these two guys — Bilal Hussein and Abdul Ameer Hussein — because they were working as professional journalists. They were the eyes of the world, covering things that the Pentagon doesn't want people in America to see."

A legitimate news organization can't help but experience a shudder at hearing that one of its employees may have been collaborating with the enemy. It's a chilling, devastating allegation. To make that charge recklessly is reprehensible.

BOB HERBERT is an Op-Ed columnist for The New York Times.

The Supreme Court's Crusade: Fairness for the Powerful

OPINION | BY ADAM COHEN | OCT. 26, 2006

WHEN JESSE WILLIAMS died of lung cancer, his widow sued Philip Morris, claiming it misled him about the danger of smoking. A jury agreed, awarding her $79.5 million in punitive damages. The Oregon Supreme Court affirmed the award, calling Philip Morris's decades of deception "extraordinarily reprehensible."

The United States Supreme Court is hearing arguments in the case next week, and the broader business community has joined Philip Morris in asking the court to sharply reduce the damages. They are relying on a controversial line of recent cases in which the court struck down punitive damages awards that it deemed "excessive."

The Philip Morris case will tell us a lot about the John Roberts court, which may be the most pro-business court in decades. It is a test of whether the court will abandon its conservative principles to be activist and "rights-making" when the party that needs help is a large corporation. It will also reveal whether the court will continue on its current disturbing path of giving corporations more protection from excessive punishment than it gives to people.

The court began its punitive damages crusade in 1996, in the case of a man who sued BMW for failing to tell him that the new car he bought had been damaged and repainted. The man won $4,000 in compensatory damages and $2 million in punitive damages. The Supreme Court set aside the punitive damages award as so "grossly excessive" that it violated due process, but the court declined to lay out any clear standards for when an award was too high.

In 2003, in a fraud case against State Farm Insurance by a policyholder, the court struck down $145 million in punitive damages. It held that the award was excessive since compensatory damages were only $1 million. That 145-to-1 ratio was unacceptable. Due process generally required, the court held, a "single-digit ratio" between punitive and compensatory damages.

These rulings are remarkably "activist" by all the traditional measures. They take a vaguely worded constitutional guarantee — that no one shall be deprived of property without "due process of law" — and translate it into a right that is not at all apparent from the words' plain meaning. They attempt to turn the guarantee into a precise mathematical formula. And they substitute the judges' worldview for that of elected officials. If Oregonians believe punitive damages are too high, their legislature can impose a legal cap.

These activist decisions, which give corporations valuable constitutional privileges, relied on the votes of conservative justices, who are supposedly skeptical of "judge-made" rights. Justices Sandra Day O'Connor and Anthony Kennedy provided key votes for BMW. Justice Kennedy wrote the State Farm "single-digit ratio" opinion, and Justice O'Connor and former Chief Justice William Rehnquist joined it.

The contrast with the court's decisions on punishment of human wrongdoers is stark. In 2003, the court considered the sad case of Leandro Andrade, a father of three who was given a minimum of 50 years in prison under California's tough "three strikes" sentencing law, for shoplifting $153.53 worth of videotapes from Kmart. He argued that his prison term violated the Eighth Amendment. The Supreme Court — in a majority joined by Justices O'Connor and Kennedy and Chief Justice Rehnquist — could find nothing excessive in the punishment.

Based on the Constitution's words, Mr. Andrade certainly had a stronger case than BMW or State Farm. The Eighth Amendment expressly bars "cruel and unusual punishments," which might reasonably be interpreted to cover imprisoning a man from age 37 to 87 for stealing $153.53. The companies claimed only that the punitive damages awards violated their "due process" rights, a far greater textual stretch.

On the issue of what is "excessive" punishment, Mr. Andrade's claim is also stronger. It is hard to see how it is excessive to make

Philip Morris, whose market capitalization is $166 billion, pay a mere $79.5 million for "extraordinarily reprehensive" and lethal conduct, but not excessive to make Mr. Andrade spend what is likely to be the entire second half of his life in prison for a petty theft.

The question of whether there should be constitutional limits on punitive damages has proved difficult to resolve, and it has caused divisions in both the court's liberal and conservative blocs. (It is one of the very few issues in which John Paul Stevens votes with corporations and Antonin Scalia votes against them.) Whatever the court decides, it should develop a constitutional theory of excessive punishment that covers human and corporate wrongdoers equally, as the Duke Law School Professor Erwin Chemerinsky and others have urged.

The current doctrines make no sense, least of all by the standards of conservative constitutional interpretation. Conservatives like to talk about the "framers' intent." The framers were deeply concerned about excessive punishment, and set forth their views on it in the Eighth Amendment. They would be perplexed that the high court they created believes their Constitution permits a father to remain in jail for 50 years for petty theft, but does not tolerate taking a fraction of the wealth from a company that kills people.

ADAM COHEN is the assistant editorial page editor for The New York Times.

Deportation and Due Process

EDITORIAL | BY THE NEW YORK TIMES | FEB. 13, 2009

IN A BIT OF MISCHIEF in his final days in office, the outgoing attorney general, Michael Mukasey, ruled that immigrants have no constitutional right to effective legal representation in deportation hearings. As a result, immigrants who lose their deportation hearings because their lawyer did a bad job representing their case have no right to have their case reopened.

Mr. Mukasey's legally dubious ruling scrapped a 20-year-old precedent in the handling of deportation hearings, which are held in special immigration courts overseen by the Justice Department.

Mr. Mukasey left those facing possible expulsion from the country — including longtime residents with children here and compelling claims to stay — with no remedy for the all-too-common errors committed by incompetent or inattentive lawyers. Vacating the 11th-hour strike deserves a high place on Attorney General Eric Holder's to-do list.

Mr. Mukasey was correct when he said the Sixth Amendment right to a lawyer applies only in criminal cases — and deportation is a civil action. The government also is not required to provide a lawyer to an indigent immigrant who has a case to make before a judge. That, we believe, should be changed.

But the real issue is that when a removal proceeding is prejudiced by the mistakes of a privately retained attorney, the due process clause, part of the 5th and 14th Amendments, is plainly violated. Unlike ordinary civil cases, removal actions have significant effect on an individual's liberty. Suing a derelict attorney for malpractice is not an adequate remedy.

Mr. Mukasey's cramped view of due process runs counter to the prevailing view of most federal appeals courts. Happily, Mr. Holder pledged during his recent confirmation hearing to re-examine Mr. Mukasey's policy.

By acting promptly to restore the rules to where they were before Mr. Mukasey's last-minute change, Mr. Holder can help avoid injustice — and sweep past one of the unfortunate legacies of the Bush years.

U.S. Approval of Killing of Cleric Causes Unease

BY SCOTT SHANE | MAY 13, 2010

WASHINGTON — The Obama administration's decision to authorize the killing by the Central Intelligence Agency of a terrorism suspect who is an American citizen has set off a debate over the legal and political limits of drone missile strikes, a mainstay of the campaign against terrorism.

The notion that the government can, in effect, execute one of its own citizens far from a combat zone, with no judicial process and based on secret intelligence, makes some legal authorities deeply uneasy.

To eavesdrop on the terrorism suspect who was added to the target list, the American-born radical cleric Anwar al-Awlaki, who is hiding in Yemen, intelligence agencies would have to get a court warrant. But designating him for death, as C.I.A. officials did early this year with the National Security Council's approval, required no judicial review.

"Congress has protected Awlaki's cellphone calls," said Vicki Divoll, a former C.I.A. lawyer who now teaches at the United States Naval Academy. "But it has not provided any protections for his life. That makes no sense."

Administration officials take the view that no legal or constitutional rights can protect Mr. Awlaki, a charismatic preacher who has said it is a religious duty to attack the United States and who the C.I.A. believes is actively plotting violence. The attempted bombing of Times Square on May 1 is the latest of more than a dozen terrorist plots in the West that investigators believe were inspired in part by Mr. Awlaki's rhetoric.

"American citizenship doesn't give you carte blanche to wage war against your own country," said a counterterrorism official who discussed the classified program on condition of anonymity. "If you cast your lot with its enemies, you may well share their fate."

President Obama, who campaigned for the presidency against George W. Bush-era interrogation and detention practices, has implicitly invited moral and legal scrutiny of his own policies.

But like the debate over torture during the Bush administration, public discussion of what officials call targeted killing has been limited by the secrecy of the C.I.A. drone program. Representative John F. Tierney, who on April 28 held the first Congressional hearing focused on the lawfulness of targeted killing, said he was determined to air the contentious questions publicly and possibly seek legislation to govern such operations.

The reported targeting of Mr. Awlaki "certainly raises the question of what rights a citizen has and what steps must be taken before he's put on the list," said Mr. Tierney, Democrat of Massachusetts and chairman of a House subcommittee on national security.

Counterterrorism officials, with the support of Democrats and Republicans in Congress, say the drone missile strikes have proved to be an extraordinarily successful weapon against militants in the tribal areas of Pakistan, the location of all the known C.I.A. strikes except one in Yemen in 2002. By their count, the missiles have killed more than 500 militants since 2008, and a few dozen nearby civilians.

In the fullest administration statement to date, Harold Koh, the State Department's legal adviser, said in a March 24 speech the drone strikes against Al Qaeda and its allies were lawful as part of the military action authorized by Congress after the Sept. 11, 2001, attacks, as well as under the general principle of self-defense. By those rules, he said, such targeted killing was not assassination, which is banned by executive order.

But the disclosure last month by news organizations that Mr. Awlaki, 39, had been added to the C.I.A. kill list shifted the terms of the legal debate in several ways. He is located far from hostilities in Afghanistan and Pakistan, where the perpetrators of 9/11 are believed to be hiding.

He is alleged to be affiliated with a Yemeni branch of Al Qaeda. Intelligence analysts believe that only recently he began to help plot strikes, including the failed attempt to bomb an airliner on Dec. 25.

Most significantly, he is an American, born in New Mexico, arguably protected by the Fifth Amendment's guarantee not to be "deprived of life, liberty, or property, without due process of law." In a traditional war, anyone allied with the enemy, regardless of citizenship, is a legitimate target; German-Americans who fought with the Nazis in World War II were given no special treatment.

But Ms. Divoll, the former C.I.A. lawyer, said some judicial process should be required before the government kills an American away from a traditional battlefield. In addition, she offered a practical argument for a review outside the executive branch: avoiding mistakes.

She noted media reports that C.I.A. officers in 2004 seized a German citizen, Khaled el-Masri, and held him in Afghanistan for months before acknowledging that they had grabbed the wrong man. "What if we had put him on the kill list?" she asked.

Another former C.I.A. lawyer, John Radsan, said prior judicial review of additions to the target list might be unconstitutional. "That sort of review goes to the core of presidential power," he said. But Mr. Radsan, who teaches at the William Mitchell College of Law in St. Paul, said every drone strike should be subject to rigorous internal checks to be "sure beyond a reasonable doubt" that the target is an enemy combatant.

As for the question of whether Mr. Awlaki is a legitimate target, Mr. Radsan said the cleric might not resemble an American fighting in a Nazi uniform. "But if you imagine him making radio speeches for the Germans in World War II, there's certainly a parallel," he said.

Beyond the legal debate is the question of whether killing Mr. Awlaki would be a good idea. Many Muslim activists and scholars say it would accord him martyr status and amplify his violent message. Mohamed Elibiary, a Muslim community advocate in Texas who advises law enforcement on countering extremism, said helping the

Yemeni authorities arrest Mr. Awlaki would make more sense. "I'm not saying this guy shouldn't be treated as an enemy," Mr. Elibiary said. "But there are smarter and stupider ways of eliminating your enemy."

American officials say an arrest may not be possible. "If we need to stop dangerous terrorists who hide in remote parts of the world, inaccessible to U.S. troops, law enforcement, or any central government," said the counterterrorism official, "what do you do — cover your ears and wait for a truly devastating explosion in Times Square?"

Awlaki Killing Incites Criticism on Left and Libertarian Right

THE LEDE | BY J. DAVID GOODMAN | SEPT. 30, 2011

The Lede is a blog that remixes national and international news stories — adding information gleaned from the Web or gathered through original reporting — to supplement articles in The New York Times and draw readers in to the global conversation about the news taking place online.

FOR CIVIL LIBERTARIANS, the killing of the radical cleric Anwar al-Awlaki was not a triumph for a military approach to terrorism but rather an example of its greatest shortcoming: a lack of due process.

As my colleague Scott Shane reports, some legal authorities are deeply uneasy at the notion that the government can kill an American with no judicial process and far from a combat zone.

That uneasiness was shared on Friday by those across the political spectrum, from Representative Ron Paul, the Republican of Texas who is running for president, to the liberal blogger Glenn Greenwald.

"Al-Awlaki was born here, he's an American citizen, he was never tried or charged for any crimes," Mr. Paul said, according to a CNN report. "To start assassinating American citizens without charges — we should think very seriously about this."

Mr. Paul criticized President Obama for the deadly drone strike on Mr. Awlaki's convoy, saying the suspected terrorist should have been put on trial for his alleged crimes and, if convicted, sentenced to death — as was done in the case of the Oklahoma City bomber, Timothy McVeigh.

On his blog on Salon.com, Mr. Greenwald wrote on Friday that "after several unsuccessful efforts to assassinate its own citizen, the U.S. succeeded today." He bemoaned what he guessed would be the likely response of Americans to the news of Mr. Awlaki's death:

> *What's most striking about this is not that the U.S. government has seized and exercised exactly the power the Fifth Amendment was*

designed to bar ("No person shall be deprived of life without due process of law"), and did so in a way that almost certainly violates core First Amendment protections (questions that will now never be decided in a court of law). What's most amazing is that its citizens will not merely refrain from objecting, but will stand and cheer the U.S. government's new power to assassinate their fellow citizens, far from any battlefield, literally without a shred of due process from the U.S. government.

Wonder how the power to assassinate US citizens without due process would look in the hands of Rick Perry or Michelle Bachmann

— Glenn Greenwald (@ggreenwald) Sept. 30, 2011

Mr. Awlaki's death appears to be the first targeted killing of an American citizen, as Mr. Greenwald writes. But Mother Jones magazine points out that he is not the first American to be killed in a drone strike against Al Qaeda. Kamal Derwish, a Qaeda member from outside Buffalo, N.Y., was killed in Yemen in 2002. At the time, a Bush administration official told The Times that it did not know before the attack that the 29-year-old Mr. Derwish was in the car. But administration officials made it clear that they were not troubled that he was, because he was considered a Qaeda operative and therefore a legitimate target.

The Washington Post reported in January 2010 that "the military's Joint Special Operations Command maintains a target list that includes several Americans."

"In recent weeks," the Post said, "U.S. officials have said that the government is prepared to kill U.S. citizens who are believed to be involved in terrorist activities that threaten Americans."

In December 2010, a federal judge threw out a lawsuit by Mr. Awlaki's father seeking to prevent his son's killing by American forces. (The judge noted the case raised questions about whether the president could "order the assassination of a U.S. citizen without first affording him any form of judicial process whatsoever, based on the mere assertion that he is a dangerous member of a terrorist organization." But he dismissed the case, saying Mr. Awlaki's father did not have standing to sue.)

In a post after the Post report, Mr. Greenwald pointed approvingly to an executive order signed by President Ronald Reagan in 1981 that prohibited assassinations of all kinds by the United States.

The American Civil Liberties Union on Friday objected to the killing of Mr. Awlaki, saying it "violates both U.S. and international law," according to a post on The Hill blog. The group had previously objected to Mr. Awlaki's placement on the list of those targeted for killing. "It is a mistake to invest the president — any president — with the unreviewable power to kill any American whom he deems to present a threat to the country," said Jameel Jaffer, the deputy legal director for the A.C.L.U.

Some observers found a useful comparison between the targeted killing of Mr. Awlaki and the execution of Troy Davis in Georgia last week for the 1989 murder of a police officer. (The death sentence in that case drew a chorus of criticism from abroad, especially in Europe.)

"U.S. (and U.K. liberals) got so worked up over death penalty for Troy Davis. Will we see the same anger now about Awlaki's execution?" wrote Mehdi Hasan, editor of The New Statesman, a left-leaning British magazine, on Twitter. "Doubt it."

Josh Shahryar, a writer and human rights activist, echoed the caustic sentiment of some who believe Mr. Davis was himself denied due process:

How do you expect anyone to give a rip about "due process" in the case of Awlaki when Troy Davis didn't get any 'o that? cc: @ggreenwald

— Josh Shahryar (@JShahryar) Sept. 30, 2011

Restoring Due Process

EDITORIAL | BY THE NEW YORK TIMES | JAN. 12, 2013

THE SUPREME COURT this week will consider whether to reverse a troubling 2002 decision that allowed judges greater sentencing power in certain circumstances. For the sake of fairness and consistency, it should overturn that 10-year-old ruling.

The question raised in the case to be argued Monday, Alleyne v. United States, is whether a trial judge can increase a defendant's prison term beyond a mandatory minimum sentence if the facts allowing for the longer sentence were not proved beyond a reasonable doubt.

This has been a murky area of sentencing law, made confusing by the Supreme Court's contradictory rulings. The justices ruled in 2000 that any factual determination that allows a sentence to be increased beyond the statutory *maximum* must be proved to a jury beyond a reasonable doubt. But in the 2002 case, Harris v. United States, the court said that this principle did not apply if the increase was added to a mandatory *minimum*. In that situation, the justices said, a judge could do what a statute directed, "give specific weight to certain facts when choosing the sentence," without a finding by a jury.

In the new case, Allen Alleyne was convicted of robbery and of using or carrying a firearm during the robbery. But the jury acquitted him of brandishing the gun during the robbery. Nevertheless, a judge found — by a preponderance of the evidence, a lower standard of proof — that Mr. Alleyne reasonably foresaw that his accomplice would brandish a gun. In addition to a 46-month sentence on the robbery count, the judge increased his sentence by seven years instead of by the minimum sentence of five years for carrying a gun.

Because the increased term means a greater deprivation of the defendant's liberty, the constitutional rights to due process and trial by jury require that a jury determine the facts on which the increase depends.

Those rights have been eroded by two major reforms by Congress beginning in the 1980s: the federal sentencing guidelines, which called for specific sentences for specific crimes; and mandatory minimum sentences, which give enormous power to prosecutors to determine sentences through the charges they bring.

But since 2005, the Supreme Court has ruled that the guidelines can only be advisory, because requiring judges to follow them violates a defendant's Sixth Amendment right to have a jury find the facts as a basis for sentences.

By reversing Harris, the court would be bolstering Sixth Amendment rights and restoring a role that the Constitution gives the jury.

A 5-4 Ruling, One of Three, Limits Silence's Protection

BY ADAM LIPTAK | JUNE 17, 2013

WASHINGTON — The Supreme Court issued three 5-to-4 decisions on Monday. One limited a criminal suspect's right to remain silent before being taken into custody. Another granted additional discretion to judges in sentencing. The third allowed a lawsuit against trial lawyers who had solicited clients using information from motor vehicle departments to move forward. The justices also agreed to hear a case on fair-housing laws.

RIGHT TO REMAIN SILENT The court ruled that a suspect's failure to answer a police officer's questions before an arrest may be used against the suspect at trial.

The Supreme Court has long said the Fifth Amendment's protection against self-incrimination applies after arrest and at trial. But it had never decided, in the words of a 1980 decision, "whether or under what circumstances pre-arrest silence" in the face of questioning by law enforcement personnel is entitled to protection.

The case decided Monday, Salinas v. Texas, No. 12-246, arose from the 1992 murder of two brothers, Juan and Hector Garza, in Houston. Among the evidence the police found were discarded shotgun shells.

The police questioned Genovevo Salinas, who was said to have attended a party at the Garzas' apartment. Mr. Salinas answered questions for almost an hour but would not say if a shotgun the police had taken from his home would match the recovered shells.

At trial, a prosecutor commented on Mr. Salinas's silence about the shells. "An innocent person," the prosecutor told the jury, "is going to say: 'What are you talking about? I didn't do that. I wasn't there.' He didn't respond that way. He didn't say, 'No, it's not going to match up.' "

Mr. Salinas was convicted and sentenced to 20 years in prison.

The justices in the majority on Monday offered differing rationales for sustaining the conviction. Justice Samuel A. Alito Jr., joined by Chief Justice John G. Roberts Jr. and Justice Anthony M. Kennedy, said Mr. Salinas had to expressly invoke his right to remain silent to benefit from it.

Justice Clarence Thomas, joined by Justice Antonin Scalia, wrote that "Salinas's claim would fail even if he had invoked the privilege."

Justice Stephen G. Breyer, joined by Justices Ruth Bader Ginsburg, Sonia Sotomayor and Elena Kagan, said allowing "a prosecutor to comment on a defendant's constitutionally protected silence would put that defendant in an impossible predicament." Mr. Salinas's choice, Justice Breyer wrote, was "between incrimination through speech and incrimination through silence."

SENTENCING The court overruled a 2002 decision that had required judges to impose mandatory minimum sentences even if they were not supported by jury findings. Justice Thomas, joined by the court's four liberal members, said the case could not be reconciled with a line of precedent since 2000 that gave juries a larger role in sentencing proceedings.

Justice Breyer was in the majority in the 2002 ruling, Harris v. United States, but since then has expressed ambivalence about his vote. In his 2002 concurrence, he wrote that the logic of the seminal 2000 decision, Apprendi v. New Jersey, required the opposite result. But, he added, "I cannot yet accept its rule." On Monday, he came to accept it.

The case concerned Allen R. Alleyne, who was convicted of robbery and a gun charge. The jury failed to find that Mr. Alleyne had brandished a gun, a determination that would have required a seven-year mandatory sentence. But the judge did find that it was more likely than not that Mr. Alleyne had brandished a weapon, raised the sentencing floor to seven years from five and sentenced the defendant to the longer term.

The five opinions in the decision, Alleyne v. United States, No. 11-9335, were partly about the jury's role in sentencing, with Justice

Thomas writing that there should be no difference between facts supporting an increase in the maximum sentence and facts supporting the increase in a minimum sentence. Both required jury findings, he said.

The justices also argued about respect for precedent, which Justice Thomas said was "at its nadir in cases concerning procedural rules that implicate fundamental constitutional protections."

In dissent, Justice Alito wrote that "the court's decision creates a precedent about precedent that may have greater precedential effect than the dubious decisions on which it relies."

PRIVACY The court ruled that trial lawyers in South Carolina ran afoul of part of the federal Driver's Privacy Protection Act by using information obtained from the state motor vehicles department to solicit clients for a lawsuit about overcharges from car dealerships.

The part of the federal law that permitted the lawyers to use driver information "in connection with" or "in anticipation of litigation" did not apply to solicitations, Justice Kennedy wrote for the majority. He was joined by Chief Justice Roberts and Justices Thomas, Breyer and Alito.

In dissent, Justice Ginsburg said the law, properly interpreted, allowed information to be used in "a concrete civil action between identified parties that is ongoing or impending."

She added that the decision, in Maracich v. Spears, No. 12-25, "exposes lawyers whose conduct meets state ethical requirements to huge civil liability and potential criminal liability."

FAIR HOUSING The court agreed to decide whether suits under the Fair Housing Act require proof that the challenged practice was motivated by an intent to discriminate. The appeals court in the case, Mount Holly v. Mount Holly Gardens Citizens in Action, No. 11-1507, ruled that proof of disparate impact without evidence of an intent to discriminate was enough to allow the suit to proceed.

The Father of the 14th Amendment

OPINION | BY GERARD N. MAGLIOCCA | SEPT. 17, 2013

IN SEPTEMBER 1863, the Ohio politician John Bingham was at the lowest point of his career. He had once been among the fastest-rising stars in American politics. Nine years earlier, he was among the first group of Republicans elected to the House of Representatives. Shortly after arriving in Washington, he established himself as one of the leading congressional voices against slavery. He was one of the new President Lincoln's most steadfast supporters and a key member of the House's pro-war caucus.

But things soon turned difficult. Bingham's Ohio district was redrawn after the 1860 census. Meanwhile, support for the war was flagging in the North, and soldiers at the front were not allowed to vote with absentee ballots. As a result, Bingham was drummed out of Congress during the 1862 elections.

Despite this personal and professional setback, Bingham remained confident about his future and of Union victory. The political views he espoused in Congress, he believed, would triumph; though currently unpopular, they would return to public favor in time — and with them, his own career. He told Treasury Secretary Salmon P. Chase that the "limitations of the Constitution upon the States in favor of the personal liberty of all of the citizens of Republic black & white [are] soon to become a great question before the people."

Bingham was right. Three years later, he was back in the House, elected in the wave of pro-Lincoln sentiment that swept the country in the fall of 1864. Once there, Bingham went to work. He took the lead in framing the 14th Amendment of the Constitution, and he authored its guarantee that no state shall "deny to any person within its jurisdiction the equal protection of the laws." More than any man except Abraham Lincoln, John Bingham was responsible for establishing what the Civil War meant for America's future.

Bingham was born in Pennsylvania in 1815. His mother died when he was 12 years old, and he was sent to Ohio to live with his uncle. In 1835, he enrolled at nearby Franklin College, a haven for abolitionists led by a member of the Underground Railroad. One of Bingham's classmates at Franklin was Titus Basfield, an ex-slave who was one of the first African-Americans to receive a college degree in Ohio. Bingham and Basfield became friends and corresponded regularly for the next 40 years. It was highly unusual to attend a racially integrated school in the 1830s, and Bingham's relationship with Basfield almost certainly influenced his opposition to slavery and his belief in racial equality.

Prior to his election to Congress, Bingham practiced law in eastern Ohio and was active in the Whig Party. In 1848 he served as a delegate at the Whig National Convention and became a lightning rod by attempting to introduce a platform plank that would commit Whig candidates to resist any extension of slavery to the territories. While Bingham was not yet an out-and-out abolitionist — he supported the Compromise of 1850 — he forged bonds with other leaders who would play a pivotal role in winning the Civil War. Edwin M. Stanton, a Democratic lawyer who became Lincoln's secretary of war, was one of Bingham's business competitors and a friendly political opponent. Salmon Chase, part of Lincoln's "Team of Rivals," was Bingham's mentor in the antislavery cause in Ohio. These three men would be at the center of the impeachment trial of President Andrew Johnson in 1868, with Chief Justice Chase presiding over the Senate, Bingham giving the closing argument for the House and War Secretary Stanton's dismissal by the president serving as the focus of the trial.

When the Kansas-Nebraska Act destroyed the Whig Party in 1854, Bingham seized his chance and was elected to Congress as a member of the new Republican Party. He rose to national attention during the debate over the statehood application of "Bleeding Kansas," displaying the talent that led many of his colleagues to describe him as the most eloquent member of the House. In a series of speeches over the next few years, Bingham laid out his view that the Constitution was "based upon the equality of the human race. Its primal object must be to protect each human being within its jurisdiction in the free and full enjoyment of his natural rights." In a different speech, he said: "You will search in vain in the Constitution of the United States ... for that word white, it is not there ... The omission of this word — this phrase of caste — from our national charter, was not accidental, but intentional." He added, "Black men ... helped to make the Constitution, as well as to achieve the independence of the country by the terrible trial of battle."

Bingham backed Chase for the Republican presidential nod in 1860, but he became one of Lincoln's most loyal supporters. He called the president "the saddest man I ever met," but said "few men could illustrate a point better than Lincoln by a homely story. There was always playful humor about him which seemed to be thoroughly incorporated in his nature, as a kind of offset against his constitutional sorrow and sadness."

When the secession crisis began, Bingham worried that Lincoln would not stand firm, as "the press is full of everything for compromise and carefully excludes every word said against compromise" under the slogan "compromise the Constitution, betray Liberty, and lose the African." As he told the House, "What just cause of complaint has the South, or any portion of her people, against this Government? There is none." The only injustice that could justify a revolt was that "wrong which dooms four million men and their descendants forever to abject servitude."

The Civil War transformed Bingham from a dissenter into a legislator. In the 37th Congress, from 1861 to 1863, he was instrumental in drafting bills to support the war effort, including the muster of the state militias, the admission of West Virginia and the suspension of habeas corpus. He made an impassioned plea for the successful abolition of slavery in the District of Columbia, commenting that the legislation "illustrates the great principle that this day shakes the throne of every despot upon the globe, and that is, whether man was made for government or government made for man."

While Bingham was a civil libertarian who argued after the war that the entire Bill of Rights should be extended to the acts of state governments, during the war he argued that the First Amendment did not protect any man who "encourages armed rebellion against the Constitution and laws of the Republic." Likewise, he said that the Fifth Amendment's guarantee that "no person shall be deprived of life, liberty, and property, without due process of law" was the "law of peace, not of war. In peace, that wise provision of the Constitution must be, and is, enforced by the civil courts; in war, it must be, and is, to a great extent, inoperative and disregarded."

President Lincoln recognized Bingham's ability and offered him several jobs after the congressman was defeated in 1862. Bingham turned down a judgeship in Florida and a post as the administration's top lawyer at the Court of Claims, but Lincoln would not take no for an answer. In 1864, the president asked him to lead the prosecution of the surgeon general in a court martial. Bingham hesitated because he knew nothing about military law, but Lincoln convinced him by saying that no "common lawyer understands martial or military law, but I think that you can learn it as soon as any man I know." When the president was assassinated, Bingham vindicated that faith by serving as one of the three military prosecutors of John Wilkes Booth's co-conspirators, where he gave the closing argument in one of the most sensational trials of the 19th century.

Bingham won back his congressional seat in 1864, and a year later he received a coveted position on the Joint Committee on Reconstruction, which was charged with setting the conditions for the South's return to the Union. In the 39th Congress he vied with Thaddeus Stevens for the leadership of the House and largely prevailed in his view that the rebel states should remain under military occupation until they agreed to ratify a new constitutional amendment.

Most significantly, Bingham drafted the crucial language of that 14th Amendment. It is Bingham who is responsible for the words: "No state shall make or enforce any law which shall abridge the privileges or immunities of citizens of the United States; nor shall any state deprive any person of life, liberty, or property, without due process of law; nor deny to any person within its jurisdiction the equal protection of the laws."

This sentence would be the legal basis for the Supreme Court's subsequent decisions desegregating the public schools, securing equality for women, and creating the right to sexual privacy. Bingham also said that his text would also extend all of the protections of the Bill of Rights to the actions of state governments, which is largely, though not completely, the law today.

When the ex-Confederate States refused to ratify the 14th Amendment, Bingham crafted a legislative compromise that ordered the Union Army to organize new elections across the South that would include African-Americans. He told the House that "unless you put [the South] in terror of your laws, made efficient by the solemn act of the whole people to punish the violators of oaths, they will defy your restricted legislative power when reconstructed."

Sadly, of course, this kind of bitter resistance was the norm until The Rev. Dr. Martin Luther King Jr. led the civil rights movement to victory in the 1960s, but Bingham did his best to prevent that outcome. The new state elections organized under the Military Reconstruction Acts led to the ratification of the 14th Amendment in 1868, and Bingham played a central role in shaping the Ku Klux Klan Act of 1871, which was intended to stop racist vigilantes and is now a cornerstone of civil rights law.

Bingham remained in Congress until 1873, and then served as the American ambassador to Japan for 12 years before retiring to Ohio. He died in 1900, largely forgotten.

Bingham's legacy is best summarized by a speech that he gave as a young man. In it, he said: "When the vital principle of our government, the equality of the human race, shall be fully realized, when every fetter within our borders shall be broken … and a noble mission fulfilled, we may call to the down-trodden and oppressed of all lands — come."

GERARD N. MAGLIOCCA is a professor of law at Indiana University and the author of "American Founding Son: John Bingham and the Invention of the Fourteenth Amendment."

End Immigration Detention

EDITORIAL | BY THE NEW YORK TIMES | MAY 15, 2015

OF ALL THE malfunctioning parts in the country's broken-down immigration machinery, probably the most indefensible is the detention system.

This is the vast network of jails and prisons where suspected immigration violators are held while awaiting a hearing and possible deportation. Immigrant detainees are not criminal defendants or convicts serving sentences. They are locked up merely because the government wants to make sure they show up in immigration court.

Detention is intended to help enforce the law, but, in practice, the system breeds cruelty and harm, and squanders taxpayer money. It denies its victims due process of law, punishing them far beyond the scale of any offense. It shatters families and traumatizes children. As

JENNIFER WHITNEY FOR THE NEW YORK TIMES

The South Texas Family Detention Facility in Dilley, Tex.

a system of mass incarceration — particularly of women and children fleeing persecution in Central America — it is immoral.

The director of Immigration and Customs Enforcement, or ICE, Sarah Saldaña, on Wednesday announced a set of reforms to the family detention system. Federal officials do this from time to time after advocates and journalists expose — as they have for years — the abuses within detention walls. Ms. Saldaña says she wants the "optimal level of care" for detainees, and so she will create a committee and give lawyers more working space to meet with clients, among other things.

But committees and cubicles won't touch the heart of the problem. It's time to end mass detention, particularly of families. Shut the system down, and replace it with something better.

A powerful case for ending immigration detention, along with an array of alternatives, is made in a new report from the United States Conference of Catholic Bishops and the Center for Migration Studies. It traces how the system has grown immense, from housing 85,000 detainees in 1995 to more than 440,000 in 2013. There are many reasons for this growth, including state and local immigration crackdowns, federal dragnet programs like Secure Communities and the flood of money from Congress to the private prison operators that have profited so fruitfully from immigrant criminalization. The system has gotten more sprawling and scandal-prone, but reforms don't stick. The notorious Hutto family detention center in Texas, where children went to classes in prison scrubs, stopped housing families. But the surge of families at the border seeking refuge last year created a political crisis and led the department to resurrect family detention, with new centers with thousands of prison beds for mothers and children.

The report points out that the detention system has become an enormous funnel for the crushingly overburdened, underfunded immigration courts, which receive a meager $300 million from Congress each year, one-sixtieth of what ICE and Customs and Border Protection get. By the end of March, nearly 442,000 cases were pending before immigration judges, with an average case waiting 599 days to be heard, and delays in some courts of more than two years. This is not efficiency or due process.

Ending mass detention would not mean allowing unauthorized immigrants to disappear. Supervised or conditional release, ankle bracelets and other monitoring technologies, plus community-based support with intensive case management, can work together to make the system more humane. But neither Congress nor the Homeland Security Department has embraced these approaches, which would be far cheaper than locking people up.

No one can expect such reforms soon from Congress, which by law requires the Department of Homeland Security to maintain, at all times, 34,000 detention beds, no matter the need. But the problem has to be acknowledged: the inhumanity and wasted expense of imprisoning people who could be working and providing for their families. The American immigration system should reflect our values. The detention system does not do that.

Publicly, We Say #MeToo. Privately, We Have Misgivings.

OPINION | BY DAPHNE MERKIN | JAN. 5, 2018

YOU CAN BE SURE that this weekend at the Golden Globes, Hollywood celebrities, not exactly known for their independent thinking, will turn the red carpet into a #MeToo moment replete with designer duds. Many have promised to wear black dresses to protest the stream of allegations against industry moguls and actors. Perhaps Meryl Streep will get grilled — again — about what she knew about Harvey Weinstein. The rest of us will diligently follow along on Twitter, sharing hashtags and suitably pious opprobrium.

But privately, I suspect, many of us, including many longstanding feminists, will be rolling our eyes, having had it with the reflexive and unnuanced sense of outrage that has accompanied this cause from its inception, turning a bona fide moment of moral accountability into a series of ad hoc and sometimes unproven accusations.

For many weeks now, the conversation that has been going on in private about this reckoning is radically different from the public one. This is not a good sign, suggesting the sort of social intimidation that is the underside of a culture of political correctness, such as we are increasingly living in.

The women I know — of all ages — have responded by and large with a mixture of slightly horrified excitement (bordering on titillation) as to who will be the next man accused and overt disbelief.

Publicly, they say the right things, expressing approval and joining in the chorus of voices that applaud the takedown of maleficent characters who prey on vulnerable women in the workplace.

In private it's a different story. "Grow up, this is real life," I hear these same feminist friends say. "What ever happened to flirting?" and "What about the women who are the predators?" Some women, including random people I talk to in supermarket lines, have gone so far as to call it an outright witch hunt.

It goes without saying that no one is coming to the defense of heinous sorts, like Kevin Spacey and Matt Lauer. But the trickle-down effect to cases like those of Garrison Keillor, Jonathan Schwartz, Ryan Lizza and Al Franken, in which the accusations are scattered, anonymous or, as far as the public knows, very vague and unspecific, has been troubling.

Perhaps even more troubling is that we seem to be returning to a victimology paradigm for young women, in particular, in which they are perceived to be — and perceive themselves to be — as frail as Victorian housewives.

Consider the fact that the campaign last month against the Met to remove a Balthus painting that shows a young girl in a suggestive light was organized by two young Manhattan feminists. Fortunately, they were unsuccessful. This is the kind of censorship practiced by religious zealots.

What happened to women's agency? That's what I find myself wondering as I hear story after story of adult women who helplessly acquiesce to sexual demands. I find it especially curious given that a majority of women I know have been in situations in which men have come on to them — at work or otherwise. They have routinely said, "I'm not interested" or "Get your hands off me right now." And they've taken the risk that comes with it.

The fact that such unwelcome advances persist, and often in the office, is, yes, evidence of sexism and the abusive power of the patriarchy. But I don't believe that scattershot, life-destroying denunciations are the way to upend it. In our current climate, to be accused is to be convicted. Due process is nowhere to be found.

And what exactly are men being accused of? What is the difference between harassment and assault and "inappropriate conduct"? There is a disturbing lack of clarity about the terms being thrown around and a lack of distinction regarding what the spectrum of objectionable behavior really is. Shouldn't sexual harassment, for instance, imply a degree of hostility? Is kissing someone in affection, however inappropriately, or showing someone a photo of a nude male torso necessarily predatory behavior?

I think this confusion reflects a deeper ambivalence about how we want and expect people to behave. Expressing sexual interest is inherently messy and, frankly, nonconsensual — one person, typically the man, bites the bullet by expressing interest in the other, typically the woman — whether it happens at work or at a bar. Some are now suggesting that come-ons need to be constricted to a repressive degree. Asking for oral consent before proceeding with a sexual advance seems both innately clumsy and retrograde, like going back to the childhood game of "Mother, May I?" We are witnessing the re-moralization of sex, not via the Judeo-Christian ethos but via a legalistic, corporate consensus.

Stripping sex of eros isn't the solution. Nor is calling out individual offenders, one by one. We need a broader and more thoroughgoing overhaul, one that begins with the way we bring up our sons and daughters.

These are scary times, for women as well as men. There is an inquisitorial whiff in the air, and my particular fear is that in true American fashion, all subtlety and reflection is being lost. Next we'll be torching people for the content of their fantasies.

DAPHNE MERKIN, a critic and novelist, is the author, most recently, of "This Close to Happy: A Reckoning With Depression."

Education Secretary Betsy DeVos Is Sued Over Sexual Assault Guidance

BY ERICA L. GREEN | JAN. 25, 2018

WASHINGTON — Victims' rights and women's rights groups sued Education Secretary Betsy DeVos on Thursday, saying that rules that she issued last year to guide campuses on how to manage sexual assault complaints violated federal law and discriminated against accusers.

Three organizations, represented by prominent civil rights litigators, filed a complaint in the Northern District of California outlining ways that the guidance issued by Ms. DeVos in the fall had had a "chilling effect" on campus sexual assault investigations.

Since the guidance was issued, the groups charged, accusers have been less inclined to pursue sexual assault cases, and colleges have demonstrated a lack of urgency and clarity in pursuing them.

In September, Ms. DeVos rescinded Obama-era guidance on how colleges should manage the investigations under Title IX, the federal law that prohibits sex discrimination and governs the rules on investigating sexual assault on campus.

A spokeswoman for the department declined to comment, citing pending litigation.

Under Ms. DeVos's administration, the department has continued to open sexual assault cases and has maintained a contentious Obama-era practice of publishing a list of campuses with open investigations.

Last week, in an abrupt and unannounced move, the department began publishing a database of all pending civil rights cases. According to the database, which is to be updated monthly, the department is investigating 773 sexual harassment cases and 480 sexual violence cases.

The Obama-era guidance, issued in 2011 and 2014, reinforced the obligation of colleges and universities to respond to sexual assault claims and was widely hailed as strengthening protections for accusers amid increasing evidence that those institutions were skirting their responsibilities to investigate sexual misconduct. But it was widely assailed by men's rights and conservative civil liberties groups as heavily biased against the accused.

In an extensive policy speech announcing the new guidance, Ms. DeVos outlined what she described as a "failed system" that violated students' due process rights and lacked public confidence.

"Schools must continue to confront these horrific crimes and behaviors head-on," Ms. DeVos said in September. "But the process must also be fair and impartial, giving everyone more confidence in its outcomes."

Ms. DeVos issued interim guidance that raised the standard of proof for accusers to "clear and convincing evidence" from a "preponderance of evidence" and allowed cases to be settled in mediation sessions between the accuser and the accused. It also dropped time frames for completing investigations.

"The new policy discriminates against women and girls and makes it harder for them to learn in a safe environment," said Fatima Goss Graves, the president of the National Women's Law Center, which is representing the litigants in the suit.

The plaintiffs in the suit, Equal Rights Advocates, SurvJustice and the Victim Rights Law Center, all advise or represent people who say they were sexually assaulted. The groups are being represented by Equal Rights Advocates, Democracy Forward Foundation, the National Center for Youth Law and the National Women's Law Center.

In the complaint, SurvJustice said that the group had not only seen "a decrease in the number of sexual violence survivors seeking its services," but also observed a trend in educational institutions not responding at all, or not responding as promptly to its clients' complaints.

The group also wrote of "students who have questioned whether they should continue with their plans to report sexual violence given the uncertainty regarding their legal protections and an anticipated lowered likelihood of success created by the policy change."

The Victims Rights Law Center, which focuses its efforts on rape and sexual assault, said Ms. DeVos's guidance was "devastating" to its mission and operational activities.

The groups are asking that the guidance be rescinded as unlawful.

"With each day that passes, this discriminatory policy will continue to cause harm to survivors of sexual harassment and violence," said Alice Y. Abrokwa, a lawyer at the National Center for Youth Law.

In their complaint, the groups wrote that Ms. DeVos and her acting leader of civil rights, Candice Jackson, made statements that revealed their bias against accusers.

They cited Ms. DeVos's policy address during which she asserted that "if everything is harassment, then nothing is," and Ms. Jackson's dismissal of women who accused President Trump of sexual harassment as "fake victims."

Due Process for Undocumented Immigrants, Explained

BY KATIE BENNER AND CHARLIE SAVAGE | JUNE 25, 2018

WASHINGTON — President Trump said on Twitter this weekend that undocumented immigrants were invaders who "must immediately, with no Judges or Court Cases," be sent home. Mr. Trump's comments prompted criticism that he wanted the United States to strip immigrants and asylum seekers of due-process rights. He also appeared to ignore the fact that some people who enter the country illegally are already removed from the United States without court hearings.

Here is what you need to know about how due process is applied in cases of illegal immigration:

WHAT IS DUE PROCESS?

Generally speaking, the Supreme Court says that due process allows people to exercise the legal rights and court processes afforded to them by American law, and it allows them to contest an action proposed by the government in front of a neutral decision maker, like a judge.

DO UNDOCUMENTED IMMIGRANTS HAVE A RIGHT TO DUE PROCESS?

Yes. Courts have consistently held that anyone on United States soil is protected by the Constitution's right to due process, even if they illegally entered the country, though people generally have greater legal protections inside the country than at the border.

How much process is deemed to be "due" depends on the situation. Courts have upheld that people who entered the United States illegally and were ordered deported have a right to appeal those decisions. But the courts have also essentially said that Congress can decide that more limited procedures are sufficient for noncitizens detained at the border.

WHAT KIND OF DUE PROCESS DO UNDOCUMENTED IMMIGRANTS GET?

Immigrants ordered to leave the country can fight deportation through civil proceedings involving immigration courts and judges overseen by the Justice Department. They can present testimony and evidence before an immigration judge, akin to a trial. They can be represented by a lawyer and can appeal unfavorable decisions to the Board of Immigration Appeals, an arm of the Justice Department.

Even if immigrants are ordered deported by the immigration appeals board, they can challenge those rulings again in front of a federal court. The process can take months or even years, especially because there is a significant backlog of such cases.

CAN THE GOVERNMENT BYPASS THAT PROCESS?

Yes. A 1996 statute permits immigration authorities to deport people without a hearing, a lawyer or a right of appeal under certain conditions,

TAMIR KALIFA FOR THE NEW YORK TIMES

Undocumented immigrants arriving Sunday in McAllen, Tex., after being processed by Customs and Border Protection and released.

a process known as expedited removal. Under current policy, the Department of Homeland Security criteria for expedited removals apply to undocumented migrants found within 100 miles of the border and within 14 days of entering the country. The statute imposes no geographic limit and allows for expedited removals up to two years after a migrant has entered the country, raising the possibility that the Trump administration may use this power more aggressively.

CAN A NEW IMMIGRANT AVOID EXPEDITED REMOVAL?

Yes, by seeking asylum. When that happens, officers at the United States Citizenship and Immigration Services — not a judge — will review cases to decide whether applicants have a credible fear of persecution back home. If so, they are placed in the immigration court system for a fuller consideration of their request. If officers decided that asylum seekers have no credible fear and should be deported, they still have a right to appeal that denial to an immigration judge, who has seven days to decide.

WHAT ABOUT 'ZERO TOLERANCE' AND CRIMINAL PROSECUTION?

Further complicating matters, while asylum and deportation proceedings are a civil process, the government can also separately pursue criminal prosecution in regular federal court. Illegally entering the United States is a misdemeanor on the first offense and a felony for repeat offenders. In April, Attorney General Jeff Sessions announced a "zero tolerance" policy for such crimes.

HOW DOES THIS RELATE TO FAMILY SEPARATION?

The systematic practice of handing adults to the custody of United States marshals for criminal prosecution separated families because their children cannot be held in custody and thus were considered unaccompanied. Immigration authorities then send the children to the Health and Human Services Department.

After Mr. Trump signed an executive order last week aimed at ending the separation of families by detaining parents and children together indefinitely, the Homeland Security Department stopped transferring adults with children to the marshals, creating a temporary reprieve.

WHAT ABOUT 'CATCH AND RELEASE'?

Separate from its zero-tolerance policy of prosecuting all adults who enter the country illegally, the Trump administration has also sought to end so-called catch and release. Under that practice, adult migrants are paroled into the country while their lengthy asylum and deportation proceedings play out.

Ending catch and release is more complicated for families who are caught trying to illegally enter the United States together. Under a 2015 court ruling, the Department of Homeland Security may hold children for only 20 days before it must turn them over to the Department of Health and Human Services for temporary placement with a foster family or in a licensed child-care facility.

The Trump administration has asked a judge to rescind that ruling so that it can hold children in indefinite immigration detention, permitting immigration authorities to both keep adults detained and keep families together.

It is not clear whether the judge will grant the administration's request, raising the possibility that family separations may resume in mid-July.

Adding to the confusion, it is not clear that the government has sufficient space to keep detaining all of the undocumented migrants apprehended near the border for now, although Mr. Trump has directed other agencies, including the Pentagon, to make space in their facilities.

America Started Over Once. Can We Do It Again?

EDITORIAL | BY THE NEW YORK TIMES | JULY 3, 2018

The editorial board represents the opinions of the board, its editor and the publisher. It is separate from the newsroom and the Op-Ed section.

PRESIDENT TRUMP PLANS to announce his second Supreme Court nominee on Monday, which also happens to be the 150th anniversary of the ratification of the 14th Amendment.

That fortuitous bit of timing offers a good opportunity to consider what might be in store for the most important amendment outside the Bill of Rights, and arguably the most consequential provision of the entire Constitution, as Justice Anthony Kennedy steps down and the court gains a solid hard-right majority that could last deep into the 21st century.

First, a little history. The original Constitution of 1787 was, for all its genius, a deeply self-contradictory document — a charter by and for a free people who enslaved hundreds of thousands of others. In 1776, America's founders declared that human equality was not only a self-evident truth, but a fundamental premise of their new nation; barely a decade later, they officially rejected that premise, writing inequality and subjugation directly into the Constitution.

Another truth soon became self-evident: If America was to survive, it would have to be reborn. That rebirth was embodied — after 80 years and a brutal civil war — in the 13th, 14th and 15th Amendments, which together represented a radical recommitment to our first and highest principles. They outlawed slavery, made the newly freed slaves American citizens and guaranteed their right to vote.

The 14th Amendment, in particular, "hit the reset button on American democracy," as Sherrilyn Ifill, director of the NAACP Legal Defense and Educational Fund, put it recently. It extended the protections in the

LEONARDO SANTAMARIA

Bill of Rights, which applied only against the federal government, to cover people in their dealings with the states. Its best known and most litigated provision, Section 1, went even further, guaranteeing for the first time the basic equality of all people, no matter their skin color, station in life or citizenship.

It's worth reading that section in full: "All persons born or naturalized in the United States, and subject to the jurisdiction thereof, are citizens of the United States and of the State wherein they reside. No State shall make or enforce any law which shall abridge the privileges or immunities of citizens of the United States; nor shall any State deprive any person of life, liberty, or property, without due process of law; nor deny to any person within its jurisdiction the equal protection of the laws."

In few enough words to fit in two tweets, the amendment's framers rejected nearly a century of American history, reshaped our democracy and mapped out the true consequences of the Civil War. They also explicitly extended the Constitution's core protections to all human beings living under the nation's laws, not only to American citizens. As the historian Eric Foner said, they were "trying to work out what it means, basically, to be a free person in the United States."

Freedom and equality — the concepts are central to the American identity, and yet for most of the last 150 years, the Supreme Court has failed to read the 14th Amendment as broadly as its framers intended. It took a century before federal laws backed up the amendment's basic guarantees for black Americans in any meaningful way. Today its meaning is still hotly debated, at least among people on the right, which raises significant concerns in the post-Kennedy era. Whatever Justice Kennedy's other flaws, he was willing to read the 14th Amendment in line with the framers' expansive intent, especially in his decisions on gay rights and reproductive rights. Now that he's gone, what will become of the amendment?

Start with its very first sentence, which grants citizenship to anyone born or naturalized on United States soil. The clause is at the core of the amendment's meaning, yet it's long been a favorite target for anti-immigrant Republicans in Congress and some conservative legal scholars. That movement got a lift when Donald Trump jumped aboard, claiming during the presidential campaign that "the 14th Amendment is very questionable as to whether or not somebody can come over and have a baby and immediately that baby is a citizen, O.K.?" No, not O.K. In fact, birthright citizenship, as it's known, has long been settled law. That didn't stop Mr. Trump, whose campaign and presidency have been built on sympathy with white nationalism, from promising that he would get it amended out of the Constitution "in my second term."

Or take the recent, bizarre refusal by at least half a dozen of President Trump's federal judicial nominees to go on record agreeing with one of the most esteemed Supreme Court decisions of all time — Brown v. Board of Education, which outlawed racial segregation in public schools and remains the most powerful invocation of the 14th Amendment's Equal Protection Clause in the court's history. The correctness of the Brown ruling is not remotely in dispute — it got high praise from three of the court's most conservative members, Chief Justice John Roberts Jr. and Justices Samuel Alito Jr. and Neil Gorsuch, during their own confirmation hearings — yet Mr. Trump's nominees for lower courts have declined repeatedly to say whether they think it was rightly decided. They take the same peculiar line, insisting that judicial ethics bar them from commenting on any case or issue that may come before them. That's a prudent position to take on a live legal controversy. As a dodge to agreeing with a ruling like Brown, it's absurd. Even if the decision is never called into doubt, it's unnerving that they're discussing the prospect at all.

Then there's race-based affirmative action, which the Supreme Court has protected in recent years thanks mainly to Justice Kennedy, who wrote the 2016 decision allowing public universities to consider race as a factor in deciding which students to admit. The 14th Amendment's framers unquestionably approved measures like these, passing laws during the same era, like the Freedmen's Bureau Act, to give black Americans government assistance with food, clothing, jobs and education. Yet despite this history, the court's conservatives, led by Chief Justice Roberts, believe that virtually any distinction based on race violates the Equal Protection Clause and have embraced the idea of a "colorblind Constitution" to chip away at even limited efforts to improve or maintain racial diversity in schools. It doesn't appear to trouble them that these same arguments were raised, and lost, in congressional debates contemporaneous with passage of the 14th Amendment. If, as is nearly certain, Mr. Trump replaces Justice Kennedy with a justice who votes solidly with the other conservatives, the chief justice will have the votes to end affirmative action for good. (Mr. Trump isn't even waiting for the court to act, asking schools on Tuesday to stop considering race altogether in making admissions decisions.)

Finally, consider the 14th Amendment's protection of rights not listed in the Constitution itself, like a woman's right to terminate her pregnancy or a same-sex couple's right to marry and enjoy the benefits of marriage. Justice Kennedy was the key vote in both of these cases, and his departure creates a real risk that one or both could be significantly cut back.

On reproductive rights, he was the last remaining member of the three-justice plurality, all appointed by Republican presidents, who worked together in 1992 to save the central holding of Roe v. Wade. As recently as 2016, Justice Kennedy sided with the court's liberals in striking down onerous state restrictions on abortion.

He was also the court's most consistently eloquent voice in support of the equal rights of gays and lesbians, writing every landmark opinion on the issue for 20 years. The court's growing right flank appears to have little appetite for honoring the broader implications of those rulings.

The Reconstruction Amendments — the 13th, 14th and 15th — are rightly considered the nation's second founding, the beginning of a centuries-long effort to cleanse America of its original sin and to continue the work of perfecting the union. Interpreting the 14th Amendment in light of its history and original meaning — a method the conservative justices swear by in most other cases — should lead the Supreme Court to wield it much more aggressively than it has. But as an increasingly hard-right majority settles in, it's reasonable to fear that the court will move in the wrong direction for years to come.

Supreme Court Limits Police Powers to Seize Private Property

BY ADAM LIPTAK AND SHAILA DEWAN | FEB. 20, 2019

WASHINGTON — The Supreme Court ruled on Wednesday that the Constitution places limits on the ability of states and localities to take and keep cash, cars, houses and other private property used to commit crimes.

The practice, known as civil forfeiture, is a popular way to raise revenue and is easily abused, and it has been the subject of widespread criticism across the political spectrum. The court's decision will open the door to new legal arguments when the value of the property seized was out of proportion to the crimes involved.

In this case, the court sided with Tyson Timbs, a small-time drug offender in Indiana who pleaded guilty to selling $225 of heroin to undercover police officers. He was sentenced to one year of house arrest and five years of probation, and was ordered to pay $1,200 in fees and fines.

State officials also seized Mr. Timbs's $42,000 Land Rover, which he had bought with the proceeds of his father's life insurance policy, saying he had used it to commit crimes.

The Supreme Court has ruled that the Eighth Amendment, which bars "excessive fines," limits the ability of the federal government to seize property. On Wednesday, in a 9-to-0 decision that united justices on the left and right, the court ruled that the clause also applies to the states under the 14th Amendment, one of the post-Civil War amendments.

Justice Ruth Bader Ginsburg, writing for eight justices, said the question before the court was an easy one. "The historical and logical case for concluding that the 14th Amendment incorporates the Excessive Fines Clause is overwhelming," she wrote.

"For good reason, the protection against excessive fines has been a constant shield throughout Anglo-American history: Exorbitant tolls undermine other constitutional liberties," she wrote. "Excessive fines can be used, for example, to retaliate against or chill the speech of political enemies."

Quoting from an earlier decision, she wrote that even absent a political motive, "fines may be employed 'in a measure out of accord with the penal goals of retribution and deterrence,' for 'fines are a source of revenue,' while other forms of punishment 'cost a state money.' "

Justice Ginsburg also wrote that excessive fines have played a dark role in this nation's history.

"Following the Civil War," she wrote, "Southern states enacted Black Codes to subjugate newly freed slaves and maintain the prewar racial hierarchy. Among these laws' provisions were draconian fines for violating broad proscriptions on 'vagrancy' and other dubious offenses."

The decision will not halt civil forfeitures, said Wesley P. Hottot, a lawyer with the Institute for Justice, which represented the Land Rover's owner.

"People are still going to lose their property without being convicted of a crime, they're still going to have their property seized," Mr. Hottot said. "The new thing is that they can now say at the end of it all, whether I'm guilty or not, I can argue that it was excessive."

Law enforcement agencies have resisted efforts to curtail civil forfeiture, saying they rely on the proceeds for sorely needed equipment. It is difficult, if not impossible, to calculate the total value of civil forfeitures by local police departments and prosecutors, but a significant portion comes from joint operations with federal law enforcement and is tracked by the Justice Department.

In fiscal year 2018, state and local agencies received $400 million through this arrangement, known as equitable sharing. The amount varied widely by agency — the Surprise Police Department in Arizona received $570,000, while the Buffalo Police Department in upstate New York got $130,000. The New York Police Department took in $7.8 million.

In Philadelphia, forfeiture proceeds once accounted for 20 percent of prosecutors' budget, while agencies in New York and California tended to take in the highest sums, according to the Institute for Justice.

Investigations across the country have uncovered many examples where the property seized was disproportionate to the crime, taken from innocent citizens or targeted in accordance with law enforcement wish lists. As its name suggests, a civil forfeiture does not require a criminal conviction or even criminal charges but only proof that the property at issue was used in connection with a crime. Owners who wish to reclaim their property must demonstrate that it was not, or that it was used without their knowledge.

A recent series of articles by the Greenville News examined every civil forfeiture case in South Carolina from 2014 to 2016, finding examples like that of Ella Bromell, a 72-year-old woman who had to fight off the forfeiture of her home after drug dealers conducted transactions on her property, despite Ms. Bromell's multiple attempts to stop them.

In a similar case in Philadelphia, where law enforcement agencies once took in $5.6 million a year in civil forfeiture, according to the Institute for Justice, a couple's home was seized in 2014 after their son was arrested on charges of making a $40 drug sale there. A case against the city's forfeiture practices was finally settled last year.

Justice Ginsburg suggested that the effect of the ruling could be limited. "All 50 states," she wrote, "have a constitutional provision prohibiting the imposition of excessive fines either directly or by requiring proportionality." Wednesday's decision may influence how state courts interpret those provisions, and they may use them to scrutinize civil forfeitures more closely.

The Supreme Court had already ruled that most of the protections in the Bill of Rights, which originally restricted the power of only the federal government, also applied to the states under the 14th Amendment.

The court left open the question of whether the seizure of Mr. Timbs's Land Rover amounted to an excessive fine, leaving its resolution to lower courts. But Justice Ginsburg suggested that the penalty was disproportionate to the offense, writing that the vehicle was worth "more than four times the maximum $10,000 monetary fine assessable against him for his drug conviction."

Justice Clarence Thomas agreed with the result in the case, Timbs v. Indiana, No. 17-1091, but said he would have gotten to the same place by a different route.

While the majority on Wednesday relied on the due process clause of the 14th Amendment, Justice Thomas said he would have ruled "the right to be free from excessive fines is one of the 'privileges or immunities of citizens of the United States' protected by the 14th Amendment."

The difference between the two approaches was meaningful, he wrote, accusing the Supreme Court of misplaced reliance on the due process clause to establish substantive constitutional rights like ones to abortion and same-sex marriage.

Justice Thomas did not address objections to modern civil forfeiture practices on Wednesday. In a 2017 opinion, though, he wrote that "this system — where police can seize property with limited judicial oversight and retain it for their own use — has led to egregious and well-chronicled abuses." His opinion cited reporting from The Washington Post and The New Yorker.

Mr. Hottot, who argued on behalf of Mr. Timbs, said courts alone cannot address the abuses inherent in civil forfeiture.

"Police and prosecutors will continue to engage in this kind of policing for profit unless and until legislatures no longer allow them to keep 100 percent of the proceeds to forfeitures," he said.

He added that Wednesday's ruling could nonetheless bring needed scrutiny to the issue.

"Police and prosecutors have no incentive to be reasonable about what they take because they get to keep everything they take," he said. "Now we know that judges at the end of the process have to evaluate if that's really justice or not."

ADAM LIPTAK reported from Washington, and **SHAILA DEWAN** from New York.

Glossary

abridge To limit or restrain.

appeal To apply to a higher court to reverse the decision of a lower court.

defendant A person or institution accused of a crime or sued in a court of law.

deprive To deny the use of something, as a person of their rights.

detain To hold a person in jail or another facility, usually while awaiting a trial or hearing.

dissent An opinion filed by a judge or judges who held the minority view in a decision.

eminent domain The right of a government to seize private property for public use.

felony A crime more serious than a misdemeanor.

habeas corpus A writ in which a person who is being detained or imprisoned can apply to be brought before a court to argue that their imprisonment is unlawful. In Latin, literally "you have the body."

hearsay Testimony or evidence by a witness of another person's words. Because it did not come directly from the person who made the statement, it is not admissible in a court of law.

incorporate To include something within the umbrella of something else.

incrimination A statement that accuses or implicates someone in a crime.

indigent A person who is poor.

infringe To limit or restrain.

jurisdiction The power of a court; the area over or extent to which a court has authority.

lien The right to keep a person's property until a debt has been paid.

misdemeanor A less serious (and often nonviolent) crime.

plaintiff A person or institution accusing or suing another person or institution in a court of a law.

prosecution The institution in a court of law trying to prove that a crime was committed.

render To declare a verdict in a court of law.

sovereignty Power or authority of a government.

standing The right to bring a matter before a court of law.

stay A legal order to stop a judicial proceeding. Often, a stay maintains a previous decision or order while the case or related cases are appealed to another court.

Media Literacy Terms

"Media literacy" refers to the ability to access, understand, critically assess and create media. The following terms are important components of media literacy, and they will help you critically engage with the articles in this title.

attribution The method by which a source is identified or by which facts and information are assigned to the person who provided them.

balance Principle of journalism that both perspectives of an argument should be presented in a fair way.

bias A disposition of prejudice in favor of a certain idea, person or perspective.

byline Name of the writer, usually placed between the headline and the story.

caption Identifying copy for a picture; also called a legend or cutline.

chronological order Method of writing a story presenting the details of the story in the order in which they occurred.

column A type of story that is a regular feature, often on a recurring topic, written by the same journalist, generally known as a columnist.

credibility The quality of being trustworthy and believable, said of a journalistic source.

critical review A type of story that describes an event or work of art, such as a theater performance, film, concert, book, restaurant, radio or television program, exhibition or musical piece, and offers critical assessment of its quality and reception.

editorial Article of opinion or interpretation.

headline Type, usually 18 point or larger, used to introduce a story.

impartiality Principle of journalism that a story should not reflect a journalist's bias and should contain balance.

intention The motive or reason behind something, such as the publication of a news story.

inverted pyramid A method of writing a story using facts in order of importance, beginning with a lead and then gradually adding paragraphs in order of relevance from most interesting to least interesting.

motive The reason behind something, such as the publication of a news story or a source's perspective on an issue.

news story An article or style of expository writing that reports news, generally in a straightforward fashion and without editorial comment.

op-ed An opinion piece that reflects a prominent individual's opinion on a topic of interest.

paraphrase The summary of an individual's words, with attribution, rather than a direct quotation of their exact words.

quotation The use of an individual's exact words indicated by the use of quotation marks and proper attribution.

reliability The quality of being dependable and accurate, said of a journalistic source.

source The origin of the information reported in journalism.

style A distinctive use of language in writing or speech; also a news or publishing organization's rules for consistent use of language with regard to spelling, punctuation, typography and capitalization, usually regimented by a house style guide.

tone A manner of expression in writing or speech.

Media Literacy Questions

1. Compare the headlines of "Judge Parker Speaks" (on page 11) and "Marshall Heard in Frank's Behalf" (on page 20). Which is a more compelling headline, and why? How could the less compelling headline be changed to better draw the reader's interest?

2. Does Dean Dinwoodey demonstrate the journalistic principle of balance in his article "High Court Silent on Search Rights" (on page 45)? If so, how did he do so? If not, what could he have included to make his article more balanced?

3. "Due Process Under Review" (on page 110) is an example of a critical review. What is the purpose of a critical review? Do you feel this article achieved that purpose?

4. Identify the various sources cited in the article "In Search of the Source of the Right to Privacy" (on page 127). How does Tamar Lewin attribute information to each of these sources in her article? How effective are her attributions in helping the reader identify her sources?

5. In "Inmate on Release Program Deserves Due Process, High Court Says" (on page 137), Linda Greenhouse mainly paraphrases information from Justice Clarence Thomas's opinion for the Court. What are the strengths of the use of a paraphrase as opposed to a direct quote? What are the weaknesses?

6. The article "Mocking Due Process" (on page 141) is an example of an op-ed. Identify how Bob Herbert's attitude and tone help convey his opinion on the topic.

7. Analyze the authors' reporting in "Judge Steps In for Poor Inmates Without Justice" (on page 148) and "For Poor, Bail System Can Be an Obstacle to Freedom" (on page 153). Do you think one journalist is more impartial in their reporting than the other? If so, why do you think so?

8. Does "U.S. Approval of Killing of Cleric Causes Unease" (on page 171) use multiple sources? What are the strengths of using multiple sources in a journalistic piece? What are the weaknesses of relying heavily on only one or few sources?

9. Identify each of the sources in "Awlaki Killing Incites Criticism on Left and Libertarian Right" (on page 175) as a primary source or a secondary source. Evaluate the reliability and credibility of each source. How does your evaluation of each source change your perspective on this article?

10. What is the intention of the article "Due Process for Undocumented Immigrants, Explained" (on page 197)? How effectively does it achieve its intended purpose?

11. What type of story is "America Started Over Once. Can We Do It Again?" (on page 201)? Can you identify another article in this collection that is the same type of story? What elements helped you come to your conclusion?

Citations

All citations in this list are formatted according to the Modern Language Association's (MLA) style guide.

BOOK CITATION

THE NEW YORK TIMES EDITORIAL STAFF. *Due Process: Defining Fair Legal Treatment.* New York: New York Times Educational Publishing, 2021.

ONLINE ARTICLE CITATIONS

BENNER, KATIE, AND CHARLIE SAVAGE. "Due Process for Undocumented Immigrants, Explained." *The New York Times*, 25 June 2018, https://www.nytimes.com/2018/06/25/us/politics/due-process-undocumented-immigrants.html.

BRUTON, PAUL, ET AL. "Justice Black's Order: Law Professors Deny Action Raises Issue of 'Due Process.' " *The New York Times*, 12 Oct. 1962, https://www.nytimes.com/1962/10/12/archives/letters-to-the-times-justice-blacks-order-law-professors-deny.html.

COHEN, ADAM. "The Supreme Court's Crusade: Fairness for the Powerful." *The New York Times*, 26 Oct. 2006, https://www.nytimes.com/2006/10/26/opinion/26thu4.html.

COMMAGER, HENRY STEELE. "Police vs. Due Process." *The New York Times*, 16 Jan. 1949, https://www.nytimes.com/1949/01/16/archives/police-vs-due-process-liberty-against-government-the-rise-flowering.html.

DINWOODEY, DEAN. "High Court Silent on Search Rights." *The New York Times*, 3 July 1938, https://www.nytimes.com/1938/07/03/archives/high-court-silent-on-search-rights-it-has-never-decided-whether.html.

DINWOODEY, DEAN. "Supreme Court Clears Away Old Legal Tangles." *The New York Times*, 4 Apr. 1937, https://www.nytimes.com/1937/04/04/archives/supreme-court-clears-away-old-legal-tangles-they-seem-to-be-running.html.

EATON, LESLIE. "Judge Steps In for Poor Inmates Without Justice." *The New York Times*, 23 May 2006, https://www.nytimes.com/2006/05/23/us/23court.html.

ELIGON, JOHN. "For Poor, Bail System Can Be an Obstacle to Freedom." *The New York Times*, 10 Jan. 2011, https://www.nytimes.com/2011/01/10/nyregion/10bailbonds.html.

FINKELSTEIN, MAURICE. "Due Process of Law." *The New York Times*, 2 Nov. 1924, https://www.nytimes.com/1924/11/02/archives/due-process-of-law-it-is-argued-that-the-supreme-court-exceeds-its.html.

GOODMAN, J. DAVID. "Awlaki Killing Incites Criticism on Left and Libertarian Right." *The New York Times*, 30 Sept. 2011, https://thelede.blogs.nytimes.com/2011/09/30/awlaki-killing-sparks-criticism-on-left-and-libertarian-right/.

GREEN, ERICA L. "Education Secretary Betsy DeVos Is Sued Over Sexual Assault Guidance." *The New York Times*, 29 Jan. 2018, https://www.nytimes.com/2018/01/25/us/politics/betsy-devos-sexual-assault-guidelines-lawsuit.html.

GREENHOUSE, LINDA. "Court Appears Ready to Reverse a Sodomy Law." *The New York Times*, 27 Mar. 2003, https://www.nytimes.com/2003/03/27/us/the-supreme-court-texas-law-court-appears-ready-to-reverse-a-sodomy-law.html.

GREENHOUSE, LINDA. "Due Process Found to Apply Even in Temporary Holds on Property." *The New York Times*, 7 June 1991, https://www.nytimes.com/1991/06/07/us/due-process-found-to-apply-even-in-temporary-holds-on-property.html.

GREENHOUSE, LINDA. "High Court Still Groping to Define Due Process." *The New York Times*, 21 May 1990, https://www.nytimes.com/1990/05/31/us/washington-talk-high-court-still-groping-to-define-due-process.html.

GREENHOUSE, LINDA. "Inmate on Release Program Deserves Due Process, High Court Says." *The New York Times*, 3 Mar. 1997, https://www.nytimes.com/1997/03/19/us/inmate-on-release-program-deserves-due-process-high-court-says.html.

GREENHOUSE, LINDA. "Justices Insist Notice Be Given in Drug-Case Property Seizures." *The New York Times*, 14 Dec. 1993, https://www.nytimes.com/1993/12/14/us/supreme-court-roundup-justices-insist-notice-be-given-drug-case-property.html.

HERBERT, BOB. "Due Process, Bulldozed." *The New York Times*, 25 Sept. 2006, https://www.nytimes.com/2006/09/25/opinion/25herbert.html.

HERBERT, BOB. "Mocking Due Process." *The New York Times*, 14 Mar. 2002, https://www.nytimes.com/2002/03/14/opinion/mocking-due-process.html.

KROCK, ARTHUR. "Close Decision in 'Lost Citizenship' Cases." *The New York Times*, 21 Feb. 1963, https://www.nytimes.com/1963/02/21/archives/in-the-nation-close-decision-in-lost-citizenship-cases-dueprocess.html.

KROCK, ARTHUR. "The 'Due Process' Factor in the Meredith Case." *The New York Times*, 1 Oct. 1962, https://www.nytimes.com/1962/10/02/archives/in-the-nation-the-due-process-factor-in-the-meredith-case.html.

LEWIN, TAMAR. "In Search of the Source of the Right to Privacy." *The New York Times*, 14 Sept. 1991, https://www.nytimes.com/1991/09/14/us/the-thomas-hearings-in-search-of-the-source-of-the-right-to-privacy.html.

LEWIS, ANTHONY. "The Same Justice Can Be Both a 'Strict' and a 'Loose' Constructionist." *The New York Times*, 24 May 1970, https://www.nytimes.com/1970/05/24/archives/the-same-justice-can-be-both-a-strict-and-a-loose-constructionist.html.

LEWIS, ANTHONY J. "Supreme Court Extends Ruling on Free Counsel." *The New York Times*, 19 Mar. 1963, https://archive.nytimes.com/www.nytimes.com/interactive/2013/03/15/us/gideon-wainwright-original-times-article.html.

LIPTAK, ADAM. "A 5–4 Ruling, One of Three, Limits Silence's Protection." *The New York Times*, 18 June 2013, https://www.nytimes.com/2013/06/18/us/supreme-court-hands-down-three-decisions-that-are-5-to-4.html.

LIPTAK, ADAM, AND SHAILA DEWAN. "Supreme Court Limits Police Power to Seize Private Property." *The New York Times*, 20 Feb. 2019, https://www.nytimes.com/2019/02/20/us/politics/civil-asset-forfeiture-supreme-court.html.

LUBASCH, ARNOLD H. "Court Assails Holding of 2 for Year Without Trial." *The New York Times*, 30 Nov. 1986, https://www.nytimes.com/1986/11/30/nyregion/court-assails-holding-of-2-for-year-without-trial.html.

MAGLIOCCA, GERARD N. "The Father of the 14th Amendment." *The New York Times*, 17 Sept. 2013, https://opinionator.blogs.nytimes.com/2013/09/17/the-father-of-the-14th-amendment/.

MERKIN, DAPHNE. "Publicly, We Say #MeToo. Privately, We Have Misgivings." *The New York Times*, 5 Jan. 2018, https://www.nytimes.com/2018/01/05/opinion/golden-globes-metoo.html.

THE NEW YORK TIMES. "America Started Over Once. Can We Do It Again?" *The New York Times*, 3 July 2018, https://www.nytimes.com/2018/07/03/opinion/trump-supreme-court-nominee.html.

THE NEW YORK TIMES. "Civil Rights Gain in 1955 Described." *The New York Times*, 23 Jan. 1956, https://www.nytimes.com/1956/01/23/archives/civil-rights-gain-in-1955-described-defense-of-due-process-and.html.

THE NEW YORK TIMES. "Cleaners' Code Voided in Jersey." *The New York Times*, 12 Mar. 1936, https://www.nytimes.com/1936/03/12/archives/cleaners-code-voided-in-jersey-pricefixing-features-violate-due.html.

THE NEW YORK TIMES."Deportation and Due Process." *The New York Times*, 14 Feb. 2009, https://www.nytimes.com/2009/02/14/opinion/14sat3.html.

THE NEW YORK TIMES. "Due Process." *The New York Times*, 12 Mar. 1940, https://www.nytimes.com/1940/03/12/archives/due-process.html.

THE NEW YORK TIMES. "Due Process." *The New York Times*, 30 Aug. 1958, https://www.nytimes.com/1958/08/30/archives/due-process.html.

THE NEW YORK TIMES. "Due Process in Washington." *The New York Times*, 4 Aug. 1948, https://www.nytimes.com/1948/08/04/archives/due-process-in-washington.html.

THE NEW YORK TIMES. " 'Due Process of Law.' " *The New York Times*, 5 Oct. 1906, https://www.nytimes.com/1906/11/08/archives/due-process-of-law.html.

THE NEW YORK TIMES. "Due Process of Law." *The New York Times*, 26 Dec. 1921, https://www.nytimes.com/1921/12/26/archives/due-process-of-law.html.

THE NEW YORK TIMES. "End Immigration Detention." *The New York Times*, 15 May 2015, https://www.nytimes.com/2015/05/15/opinion/end-immigration-detention.html.

THE NEW YORK TIMES. "High Court Bars Death for Negro." *The New York Times*, 15 Jan. 1957, https://www.nytimes.com/1957/01/15/archives/high-court-bars-death-for-negro-finds-due-process-denied-in-alabama.html.

THE NEW YORK TIMES. "High Court Denies Frank's Last Plea." *The New York Times*, 20 Apr. 1915, https://www.nytimes.com/1915/04/20/archives/high-court-denies-franks-last-plea-not-shown-to-have-been-deprived.html.

THE NEW YORK TIMES. "High Court Rules on Rights of Aliens." *The New York Times*, 16 Nov. 1982, https://www.nytimes.com/1982/11/16/us/high-court-rules-on-rights-of-aliens.html.

THE NEW YORK TIMES. "High Court Strengthens Right to Silence at Arrest."

The New York Times, 18 June 1976, https://www.nytimes.com/1976/06/18/archives/high-court-strengthens-right-to-silence-at-arrest.html.

THE NEW YORK TIMES. "Judge Parker Speaks." *The New York Times*, 4 July 1903, https://www.nytimes.com/1903/07/04/archives/judge-parker-speaks-addresses-georgia-bar-association-on-due.html.

THE NEW YORK TIMES. "Marshall Heard in Frank's Behalf." *The New York Times*, 26 Feb. 1915, https://www.nytimes.com/1915/02/26/archives/marshall-heard-in-franks-behalf-mob-spirit-and-defendants-absence.html.

THE NEW YORK TIMES. "Miranda v. Arizona." *The New York Times*, 2 Oct. 1966, https://www.nytimes.com/1966/10/02/archives/miranda-v-arizona.html.

THE NEW YORK TIMES. "No Constitutional Right to Lie." *The New York Times*, 24 Jan. 1998, https://www.nytimes.com/1998/01/24/opinion/no-constitutional-right-to-lie.html.

THE NEW YORK TIMES. "Ohio Liquor Courts Declared Illegal." *The New York Times*, 8 Mar. 1927, https://www.nytimes.com/1927/03/08/archives/ohio-liquor-courts-declared-illegal-supreme-court-rules-costs-as.html.

THE NEW YORK TIMES. "Ouster of 4 Reds by Union Upheld." *The New York Times*, 22 Apr. 1947, https://www.nytimes.com/1947/04/22/archives/ouster-of-4-reds-by-union-upheld-justice-hammer-rejects-plea-that.html.

THE NEW YORK TIMES. "Restoring Due Process." *The New York Times*, 13 Jan. 2013, https://www.nytimes.com/2013/01/13/opinion/sunday/restoring-due-process.html.

NOSSITER, ADAM. "Civil Rights Slaying Raises Speedy-Trial Issue." *The New York Times*, 27 May 1994, https://www.nytimes.com/1994/05/27/us/civil-rights-slaying-raises-speedy-trial-issue.html.

ROSEN, JEFFREY. "A Terror Trial, With or Without Due Process." *The New York Times*, 10 Sept. 2006, https://www.nytimes.com/2006/09/10/weekinreview/10rosen.html.

SHANE, SCOTT. "U.S. Approval of Killing of Cleric Causes Unease." *The New York Times*, 14 May 2010, https://www.nytimes.com/2010/05/14/world/14awlaki.html.

SHUSTER, ALVIN. "Author in Prison Wins Court Test." *The New York Times*, 11 June 1957, https://www.nytimes.com/1957/06/11/archives/author-in-prison-wins-court-test-53-decision-orders-a-new-hearing.html.

TAYLOR, TELFORD. "Due Process Under Review." *The New York Times*, 16 Mar. 1980, https://www.nytimes.com/1980/03/16/archives/due-process-under-review-process.html.

TOMASSON, ROBERT E. "Prosecutors Here Are Divided 3 to 2 on Jury Trials for Misdemeanors Subject to a Year's Sentence." *The New York Times*, 19 Jan. 1970, https://www.nytimes.com/1970/01/19/archives/prosecutors-here-are-divided-3-to-2-on-jury-trials-for-misdemeanors.html.

WEAVER, WARREN, JR. "High Court Upsets a State's Trial Rules." *The New York Times*, 25 Feb. 1973, https://www.nytimes.com/1973/02/25/archives/high-court-upsets-a-states-trial-rules-right-to-crossexamine.html.

WOOD, LEWIS. " 'Due Process' Made an Issue." *The New York Times*, 3 Mar. 1937, https://www.nytimes.com/1937/03/07/archives/due-process-made-an-issue-the-phrase-used-in-two-amendments-to-the.html.

Index

This book is current up until the time of printing. For the most up-to-date reporting, visit www.nytimes.com.